Ride The Wind

© 2010 by Nancy DeLong

All rights reserved. No portion of this book may be reproduced, stored in a retrieval system or transmitted in any form or by any means, without the expressed written permission of the publisher. However, a reviewer may quote brief passages in a review to be printed in a newspaper, magazine, journal, or any appropriate electronic means.

First Printing - May 2010

RIDE THE WIND is fiction. Any resemblance to any person or place is purely coincidental.

ISBN: 978-0-9841689-2-7
Published by N. GLYNN PUBLISHING, LLC
P.O. Box 951414, Lake Mary, FL 32795-1414
www.nancydelong.com
Printed in the United States of America

Ride The Wind

Written By
NANCY DeLONG

Cover Art
MELINDA McCANN

Book Design
BLAZE CARTER

N. GLYNN PUBLISHING

LESLIE JOHN RAFFERTY
This one's for you!

RIDE THE WIND is the story of a young woman with her life in shambles who finds her way to the door of a 12-Step Program.

She meets a man who knows her better than she knows herself because he has traveled the same road of devastation and has the gift of many years of recovery--one day at a time. They learn about love from one another in ways that neither of them could have imagined.

The story follows the lives of Margaret Elizabeth O'Neil (Meg) and Sean Patrick MacIntosh through Meg's early years of sobriety. They find that laughter is their pathway to true love and that tears connect their souls.

And so it is with honor and humility that I share this story; and although it is based on fact, it is fiction.

Part One

A petite, attractive woman in her late twenties, slid into a booth at the back of the Friendly's Coffee Shop. Margaret Megan O'Neil, Meg, wore a stained lavender linen business suit with matching scuffed spike heels. She was a blonde haired, blue eyed looker, but her make up was overdone. She did her very best to look cool and detached as she "people watched" and wrote in her journal. Her hands trembled as she tried to drink her coffee. Her gaze was fixated on a booth occupied by a redheaded Scotsman, with a thick brogue, and his crew.

Sean Patrick MacIntosh looked young for his forty years. He was impeccably dressed in a white button down, Oxford cloth shirt, pressed jeans, and cowboy boots. He was animated and loud. He flirted with the waitress, and she was falling all over him. Disgusting, Meg thought.

Meg was conspicuously alone. She swallowed hard, closed her journal, stood up rigidly, and took stiff strides toward the door. Her head was in the air as she passed the booth in the front.

Sean saw her out of the corner of his eye.

"Hey you," he said.

Meg faltered but managed to ignore Sean.

"I'm talkin' to ya,'" he shouted.

Meg stopped and glanced his way.

"Weren't ya' at the meetin' this evenin'?

"Yes."

"Well, sit down here," he commanded.

"NO, thank you."

Sean looked Meg in the eye and said firmly, "I didn't ask ya' Lassie. I said, Sit down!"

Meg glared at Sean. One of the people in the booth got up so Meg could slide in. She squeezed in across from Sean. Meg felt her face flush; she crossed her arms defensively.

"So what's your name? Sean asked.

"Margaret Megan O'Neil."

"I'm Sean Patrick MacIntosh. M' friends call me Sean. Glad ta' meet ya.'"

Sean extended his hand across the table to her; she offered a limp handshake.

The others in the booth introduced themselves. Among them was Abbey, a petite, feisty blonde, who was well dressed and outgoing. She sat on one side of Sean. Another woman, Robin, a radiant, reddish haired gal, who seemed somewhat quieter, sat on the other. Meg remembered seeing them at the meeting.

"So how long have ya' been sober?"

"A year and a half."

Sean was puzzled by her answer. He fired up a cigarette and took a drag.

"How long have ya' been comin' ta' meetin's?"

"Tonight was my first one," she said proudly.

Sean studied her. He took another drag off his cigarette.

"Well, keep comin' back," Sean said.

The small talk began again. Meg was silent. She sighed with relief that the focus was off of her. The others were happy, joking, laughing. Meg, in contrast, was restless. The waitress brought her a coffee cup and filled it. Meg was uncomfortable, squirming in her seat. She had to use both hands to pick up the coffee cup in front of her. She took a sip, put down the cup, and looked to see if anyone noticed her shaking.

"I really have to go," she interrupted.

"In a minute. We'll all be headin' out," Sean replied.

As the group was breaking up, Sean reached in his pocket and pulled out a business card. He wrote his home phone number on it and handed it to Meg. He looked her squarely in the eyes.

"Call me. Anytime."

Meg gave him a cold stare and snatched the card from his hand. The instant the person next to her got up, she made her break and headed for the door.

She did not look back.

⁓

Meg sat at the kitchen table in her tiny apartment; her head was buried in her hands. Moving boxes were everywhere.

She remembered her first drink at 17, the night she met Warren. She had gazed up into his deep brown eyes. She had been mesmerized by his fabulous smile, and they had danced the night away. He had ordered her a drink, a sloe gin fizz; and before the evening ended, she had finished most of a bottle by herself. Warren didn't mind a bit; he drank the way she did. He quickly became the love of her life.

By the time Meg graduated from The Ohio State University with a double major, English and journalism, she was drinking every day. She landed a prestigious job as a general assignment reporter at The Daily

Herald in Detroit. She was given the Grosse Pointe beat where the Detroit blue bloods lived in their mansions along Lakeshore Drive. She spent her days at the Grosse Pointe Yacht Club on Lake St. Clair, where she mingled with the elite and got leads on news and feature stories. She immediately made a name for herself by writing an in-depth story on the Dodge family of automotive fame. It won her a nomination for a Pulitzer Prize in the Feature Writing category.

Meg loved her job. Writing came to her as naturally as breathing. She bounced into the impressive Herald office building every day and greeted her coworkers with cheerful hellos. She sat at her typewriter and knocked out copy on any story the city editor threw her way. She and a photographer would go out on breaking news stories and she would ask the tough questions. She spent her nights drinking at the Press Club across the street from her office. A veteran reporter, Doc Greene, took her under his wing, and they often shared long lunches at the Pontchartrain Wine Cellar, known for its "Cold Duck."

And no matter how much Meg drank, she never missed a deadline.

Warren came to visit often. At first, they went out to fancy restaurants, to the theatre, to concerts, to the ballet, and they always ended the evening closing one of the high end bars in Downtown Detroit. But as time passed, they would spend entire weekends never leaving her apartment unless they ran out of booze.

When she was home alone, she spent endless hours writing the great American novel. Her writing tools included a typewriter, which sat on her kitchen table and a 12 ounce crystal glass filled with Grant's Scotch on the rocks.

At the end of the night, she carried her glass into the bedroom, took a sip, set it on the night stand, and passed out on the bed. When the morning alarm blasted at 5:30 a.m., Meg was barely able to open her eyes. She would reach for the glass of Scotch and drink it down before getting out of bed.

Toward the end of her drinking, Warren had called Meg and said he had a special weekend planned for them in Bimini. When they arrived at the hotel, their first stop had been the cocktail lounge. After drinking their fill, they had ordered several bottles to be sent to the room.

Later they had gone for a walk on the beach carrying their whiskey bottles. They had held each other up as they stumbled along, trying to catch the seagulls. Meg had fallen down, and when Warren had tried to pick her up, he had fallen down, too. They had passed out on the beach, missing the magnificent sunset.

Meg remembered her final day at The Daily Herald. She had been late for work. She had rushed into the newspaper building and when she got to her desk, her boss had called her into his office. He had discussed a news article that she had written that was filled with errors. She had argued with him until he had slammed down the paper and pointed his finger at her.

"You're an alcoholic, Meg. You need help!"

"What right have you to call me that?" she had screamed.

"Because I'm an alcoholic and I haven't had a drink in ten years," he had said softly. "You won't get through today without a drink, and if you don't get help, you won't live to see your next birthday."

Meg had been livid, "Watch me!"

She had gone out the door, slamming it as hard as she could. When she got in her car, she had sobbed uncontrollably. Meg had gone home that day, gotten on her knees, and said the most powerful prayer of her life.

"I am an alcoholic. God help me."

Meg had not considered going to Alcoholics Anonymous; instead she had rented 400,000 square feet of Cobo Hall in Downtown Detroit for Super Bowl Weekend 1982. The director of the facility had drawn up a contract and she locked up the venue. She was nicknamed Superbowl Momma and her three day extravaganza was known as the Biggest Game in Town for the Biggest Game in Town. The only problem was that the weather shut down the airport and the roads into Downtown Detroit, so nobody came. She did all she could to pay people back, but eventually, she filed bankruptcy. She left Detroit and ended up back in Columbus, Ohio.

She soon found out that one of her creditors had reported her to the FBI saying she had hidden assets. Agents had been talking to everyone who had ever known her. She was sure they were coming after her, and she was terrified.

And when the pain and fear became more than she could bear, she had made the dreaded call to the Alcoholics Anonymous' "hot line" number. The woman who answered was very kind and had directed Meg to a meeting that night.

"Would you like someone to pick you up for the meeting?" she had asked Meg.

"Absolutely not! I don't want my neighbors to see me with an alcoholic," Meg had replied.

It was the Wednesday West Fifth meeting in Grandview; Meg had walked in a few minutes late. It had been an outrageous discussion meeting. The meeting started at 8 p.m., there was a smoke break at 9 p.m., and then it went on until almost 10 p.m.

She had read the 12 Steps for the first time. They were a blur to her. It seemed to be a laundry list of things she had to do and that was just not part of the plan she had.

Although the 10th Step talked about promptly admitting "wrongs" one day to day, Meg read the Step as, *"Continue to take personal inventory and when you are not perfect, promptly kill yourself."*

That made sense to her.

When the meeting leader asked if anyone was attending his or her first meeting, she had not raised her hand. After all, she had not had a drink for almost 18 months. She had been too busy getting on with her life without alcohol and drugs to waste time with these drunks. The topic of the meeting was "Gratitude," and Meg was not grateful for anything. Her life was in shambles.

She had listened as people said stupid things like, "I'm grateful I don't throw up when I brush my teeth in the morning," "I'm grateful there were green lights on the way to the meeting." Jesus, she had thought, these people are real sickos. No wonder they come to these meetings.

When it was her turn to talk, she had not given her name. She had passed.

She had been struck by the Scotsman who introduced himself.

"I'm Sean and I'm an al-key-holic. Hellooo everybody!" he said with a very thick brogue.

He seemed to be the leader of the group. People flocked around him. He was upbeat, outspoken, definitely a trouble maker, and that was just her style.

After the meeting, she had overheard Sean say to some of the others that they would meet up at Friendly's. She had followed one of the cars and Friendly's was a coffee shop that featured ice cream. It had definitely been a first for Meg; she had not known coffee shops featuring ice cream even existed. She had waited in her car until she saw Sean go in. When she went inside, she had headed to a booth in the back to avoid him.

That was Wednesday, just two days earlier, and in her Friday mail, she had gotten a notice that said she was being questioned by the FBI. She was to meet at FBI headquarters to discuss reports that she had committed bankruptcy fraud. Oh my God, she thought, the FBI believes I did it.

Meg looked up remembering Sean's business card. She dug it out of her purse and studied it. She threw it down on the table. She got up and paced the floor. She sat back down, picked up the card, picked up the phone, then slammed down the receiver. She studied the card.

She took a deep breath. She picked up the phone again and tried to dial the number. She could not. She sat there in front of the phone for a long moment. She picked up the phone with determination, dialed very slowly, and completed the number. The phone rang. She held her breath.

Sean was watching a John Wayne Western when the phone rang. His apartment was large, luxurious, and very tidy except for an overflowing ashtray and KitKat candy wrappers on the coffee table. He was munching a KitKat, drinking hot tea, and smoking. He was dressed in his John Wayne movie clothes which included a cowboy hat, a fringed leather vest over a plain white T-shirt, pajama bottoms, his holster and a real six shooter. He was barefooted and his feet were resting on the coffee table. The television was blasting. He turned down the volume with his remote and picked up the phone.

"How-dy Pilgrim," he said with a mock cowboy accent which was ridiculous with his Scottish brogue.

Sean heard Meg clear her throat.

"I said, How-dy!"

Meg's voice was shaky and almost inaudible.

"It's Margaret."

"Mar-gar-et? The al-key-holic I met the other night? How ya' doin' Little Missy?"

"Okay."

"So ya' just called to say 'howdy' at 2 a.m.?"

"Yes!" Meg's voice was laced with anger.

"Well, I'm here a watchin' a John Wayne shoot 'em up. Ever watch one?"

"No. Oh, I don't know. I better go."

"Hey, wait a minute," Sean said. "I'll pick ya' up for a meetin' tomorrow night. Give me your address."

"I don't know if..."

Sean interrupted her.

"Just give me your address, Lassie."

"294 West Fifth Avenue, Apartment 12B, but...."

He spoke over her.

"I'll pick you up a 7 p.m. sharp, an' I only toot the horn once."

Sean hung up on her and smiled.

At 7 p.m. on the dot, Sean drove up to Meg's apartment. He was in a shiny, white Lincoln Town Car with burgundy interior. He wore freshly pressed jeans, a button down white Oxford cloth shirt, cowboy boots, and a cowboy hat. He honked the horn once, then fired up a cigarette.

Sean studied Meg as she came out of her apartment and walked toward the car wearing a powder blue blouse, very tight mini-skirt with a matching jacket, and a scarf for flare. She stumbled in her spike heels as she hurried to the car. His face showed understanding and amusement. He reached across the passenger seat and opened the door for her. She got in and Sean pulled away.

"Well, Mar-gar-et, or may I call ya' Meg, you're mighty dressed up for a meetin,'" he said with a slight smile.

Meg glared at Sean.

"Meg's fine since you seem to have trouble pronouncing three syllable words," she said sarcastically, and then she added defensively, "and this is how I dress."

Sean ignored her sarcasm. Meg settled into her seat.

"We're going to a lead meetin' where someone shares his story. Are ya' feelin' better than last night?"

"I'm fine. And I was fine last night."

"Right. So, do ya' want ta' tell me what's goin' on?"

"I'd rather write about it," Meg snapped back.

"Well, since I don't have a typewriter mounted in my car, why don't ya' just tell me," Sean said with flair.

"The FBI."

"What about 'em?"

"They're investigating me," Meg bristled.

"Are ya' a hardened crim-in-al?"

"No."

"So what's the deal?"

"Someone says I have 'hidden funds.'"

"Do ya'?"

"No."

"Then don't drink and go ta' meetin's. It'll work out," Sean said, matter-of-factly.

Meg stared at Sean in disbelief, unwilling to accept this simple remedy to her monumental problem. They rode the rest of the way to the meeting in silence.

Sean and Meg walked into a large meeting room which was the fellowship hall of Holy Trinity Church. Sean was greeted warmly with hugs and laughter. He introduced Meg to several people and she offered her limp hand shake. Abbey, who Meg met at the coffee shop, gave Meg a terrific smile and walked up to her.

"Hi, I'm so glad to see you at the meeting tonight," she bubbled, then handed Meg a card and continued, "I meant to give you my number the other night, so here it is. Call me anytime."

Meg pulled back as quickly as she could and distanced herself from Abbey and the others. Sean watched her from the corner of his eye. She moved to the other side of the room. Sean saw an older, extremely handsome man, with dark hair and eyes, come up behind Meg. He was dressed in designer casual clothes. Meg's face lit up the minute she saw him. It was Warren. They talked for a minute and then they embraced. They found two seats in the back of the room and sat down.

The meeting began. Meg was preoccupied with Warren, whispering in his ear. She heard brief bits of the meeting. She heard the speaker mention the Steps, the

Traditions, and sponsorship. But one comment from the speaker caught her attention. He said, "I'm nine years sober and sometimes I still hold on by an eyelash."

Sean walked up to Meg after the meeting.

"Who's your friend?"

Meg was giddy.

"This is Warren," Meg said, "and Warren, this is Sean."

They shook hands.

"Good ta' meet ya,'" Sean said as he sized up Warren.

"You too, Sean," Warren replied arrogantly.

"You needn't bother to take me home. Warren will," Meg said.

Sean replied firmly, "I brought ya' ta' the meetin' Lassie; I'll drop ya' ta' home. What ya' do after that is up ta' you."

Meg started to protest and decided not to argue. She kissed Warren good-bye and left the meeting room with Sean.

As they rode home from the meeting, Meg was more talkative and relaxed.

"How long have ya' lived here in Columbus?" Sean asked.

"I moved back here two months ago. Columbus is my hometown."

"Where'd ya' move from?"
"Detroit."
"What kinda work do ya' do?"
"Oh, I've done different things, but what I am is a writer. I've worked as a reporter for several newspapers. Someday I want to write children's books."
"Where are ya' workin' now?"
"I've been substitute teaching since I came back, mostly high school English and journalism."
"What made ya' decide you're an al-key-holic?"
Meg was thoughtful before she answered.
"I took my last drink almost a year and a half ago. I didn't go to these stupid meetings or anything. I thought I could just stop drinking and using drugs and get on with my life. But I feel insane when I don't drink, and I act insane when I do." Then she angrily added, "I'd rather have cancer than be an alcoholic!"
Sean replied in a sure, steady tone, "Well ya' don't, so just be an al-key and like it."
Sean paused; Meg crossed her arms. They rode in silence for a time.

"After all this time, why'd ya' start comin' to meetin's?"

"The FBI thing. I just didn't know what else to do. I go for questioning in about a month."

"Questioning? For what?"

"Oh, I rented 400,000 square feet of Cobo Hall in Detroit and threw a three day party for Super Bowl weekend this past January. I had all kinds of entertainment--bands, singers, cheerleaders, cabaret shows--you know, something for everyone. It was a major flop financially. I owed alota people alota money. Then, someone said I had money hidden somewhere and I don't," Meg replied.

"Sounds like my kinda party!"

Sean looked at the road, digesting Meg's situation. He pulled up to her apartment and stopped.

Sean turned toward Meg, "So tell me about Warren."

"I've always loved Warren, before college even," Meg swooned. "We went our separate ways, but we stayed close. You know, we'd get together now and then. I hadn't seen him in over two years, since we went to Bimini together."

She looked at Sean, "Imagine, seeing him tonight. I didn't know he'd stopped drinking and he didn't know I was back in town."

"Drinkin' Buddy?" Sean asked.

"Oh yeah, plenty! And friends and lov...."

Meg's voice stopped in mid-sentence, embarrassed by her honesty. Sean dropped it, too. As Meg got out of the car, Sean leaned over and said, "Thanks for goin' to the meetin' tonight, Lassie. Give me a call."

Meg got out of the car, turned and smiled at Sean, walked to her door, and went into her apartment.

Sean watched her go.

Meg was elated to be with Warren again. They met at the coffee shop several days later and giggled at how different it was with her drinking Diet Pepsi instead of Grant's Scotch and him drinking iced tea instead of Jack Daniels.

A week went by before Meg thought about going back to a meeting. She stopped at a phone booth, pulled Sean's number out of her purse, and made a call. She scrambled for a pen and paper, jotted down an address, and hung up the phone. A few minutes later, she walked into an AA meeting room and walked up to Sean.

"Glad ya' called, Lassie, and glad ta' see ya' here," Sean smiled.

"Me too. Could we talk after the meeting?" Meg asked.

"Sure. I'll meet ya' at the coffee shop."

It was another large meeting room attached to a different church. Meg sat next to Sean. The room was loud and overcrowded with people, but everyone quieted down when the chairman began.

"Hi everybody, I'm Ron and I'm an alcoholic."

Everyone present said in unison, "Hi Ron."

Ron continued, *"This is an open meeting of Alcoholics Anonymous and all members of the community are welcome to attend. However, in keeping with our singleness of purpose, only alcoholics actually participate in our meeting. If your problem is other than alcohol, we hope that what you learn here will be helpful to your recovery, and or, understanding. Please help me open the meeting with a moment of silence followed by the Serenity Prayer."*

The topic of the meeting was: "HALT, don't get to hungry, angry lonely or tired." People commented that, in addition to not drinking, staying sober depends on eating regularly, letting go of resentments, helping others, and getting enough sleep. What odd concepts, Meg thought.

After the meeting, Sean was still talking to people when Meg left. She waited for him outside of the coffee shop and when they went in, they found a booth at the back. Meg noticed the reflection of a man outside the coffee shop window. He seemed to be watching her. Meg slid into the booth, Sean slid in next to her. She leaned into the corner of the booth and ordered a Diet Pepsi; he ordered a hot tea.

Sean fired up a cigarette, leaned back, and took a deep drag. He looked at Meg, studied her for a moment. He noticed her shakes had lessened and she was much calmer than when they first met.

He looked squarely into her eyes and gently said, "So Miss Meg, what da' ya' wanna talk about?

Meg shrugged her shoulders and avoided looking directly at Sean.

"Oh, I don't know, the Program I guess. I have some questions."

"Well, fire away," Sean said.

"For one thing, how long do I have to go to these dumb meetings?"

"Lassie, I had a love affair with Scotch whiskey every day for over thirteen years. When I got here I was down, low--a low bottom drunk. But I got the gift of desperation and found my way into the rooms of AA. Now, I've been comin' ta' these 'dumb' meetin's for almost fifteen years. We do this deal one day at a time."

The waitress brought their drinks. Meg watched as Sean added five sugars to his hot tea and stirred it vigorously.

Meg persisted, "So, when do you get to stop coming to the meetings?"

"When I stop breathin' I guess. My sponsor told me that the only valid excuse for missin' a meetin' was a funeral--my own. And I go by that, Meg, 'cause I found a way ta' get that whiskey every day ta' keep me sick, so I need to nurture what keeps me well every day."

Meg was still, thinking over what Sean had said, then she asked nervously, "Everybody talks about this 'sponsor' thing. What's that about?"

Sean fired up another cigarette.

"A sponsor's the one person ya' trust ta' tell ya' what ya' don't want ta' hear. A person ta' guide ya' through the Steps and Traditions and Concepts of Alcoholics Anonymous, startin' with the text book that we call the Big Book. It's someone a little further down the path than you are," Sean replied.

"Do you *have* to have a sponsor?"

"If ya' want ta' stay sober ya' do."

Meg squirmed. Sean watched her.

The waitress interrupted, "Can I get you anything else?"

"I'll have another pot a tea, Luv."

A group of people from the meeting came up to the table and started talking to Sean. He introduced them to Meg, but she wasn't paying any attention. She was awkwardly flirting with Sean grabbing his leg and leaning on his shoulder attempting to look cozy.

After they left, Sean lit up a cigarette and asked, "Anything else, Meg?"

"Will you be my sponsor?" Meg blurted out.

Sean was gentle, but firm, "I'll tell ya' somethin,' Lassie. Ya' don't know if ya' wanna get laid or if ya' wanna get sober. Your life depends on ya' gettin' sober. So that's what I'll help ya' do. And, that's **all** I'll help ya' do."

Meg reacted with shock and embarrassment at being found out. She pulled back and looked at Sean, speechless.

"If ya' want the sobriety I have, you'll do what I do. That means followin' directions startin' with callin' me every day. As of today, we're equal in not drinkin' for this day only. As alkies, we're both one drink away from a drunk," he paused, "But in the years I've been around, I've learned more ways ta' say no ta' that first drink, and that's what I'll share with ya.'"

Meg was quiet, she took in Sean's words and swallowed with difficulty.

Sean leaned back and lightened up, "Here's what ya' do. It's the four "absolutes" ta' stay sober: Don't drink, go ta' meetin's, read the Big Book, and worship your sponsor."

Meg laughed just a little.

"Call me in the mornin,' Meg, 7 a.m. sharp. And meet me at the Hill Street meetin' tomorrow night. It's at the Lutheran Church, corner of Hill and 21st. Be there at 7:30 p.m. sharp. Got it?"

Meg nodded yes.

They got up from the table and Sean gave Meg a reassuring squeeze and pat on the shoulder.

They walked out of Friendly's together and got in their cars. Sean waved and smiled at Meg as he pulled out of the parking lot.

Part Two

Meg followed directions to the best of her ability. She made sure she called Sean at 7 a.m. sharp every day. Warren was out of town on business, so Meg had more time to connect to meetings under Sean's unyielding guidance.

She met him at the Hill Street meeting on Thursday night and then Sean instructed her where to meet him the next night at the Friday Night North Group Speaker's Meeting.

Sean was near the door, talking with several women when Meg walked in. She thought he looked particularly dashing in a blue ruffled shirt with his jeans instead of his familiar Oxford cloth button down one.

Sean directed her to shake hands with everyone in the room.

"Everyone," she grimaced.

"Yes, everyone," he flatly replied.

She offered limp handshakes as she went around the room. She watched Sean out of the corner of her eye and saw him sit down in the middle of the room next to an attractive young woman, Lindy. They were animated and laughing. He kept the seat on the other side empty. Meg covered half of the room and slid into the seat next him. Sean whipped around to Meg, grabbed her shoulder, pulled her out of her chair, and sent her around to shake hands with the rest of the room. Meg was stunned that Sean knew she had only followed part of his directions. She scowled as she shook hands with everyone else in the room before she sat down again.

After the meeting, Sean introduced Meg to Lindy. He turned his back on Lindy as he asked Meg her plans for the rest of the evening and the next day. He told Meg where to meet him for a meeting the next night before leaving with Lindy.

Sean was speeding along in his shiny white Lincoln Town Car when the patrolman pulled him over.

"You were twenty miles over the speed limit. Slow it down."

Sean nodded his acknowledgement.

"So much for having cruise control," Sean said to Lindy as he dashed away.

―――

Two weeks later Warren got back from his road trip; Meg's focus was on him. Her fairy tale was coming true. They were sober and together. He took her to the finest restaurants in Columbus. She stayed at his place late into the night, but almost always managed her 7 a.m. call to Sean before leaving for work.

Meg wrote her feelings in letters to Sean and then mailed them. She sent one every day. That way when she called and he asked how she was she would simply say, "Fine! Did you read my letter?"

The more entrenched she became with Warren, the less connected she was to a program of recovery. It was almost a month before she and Warren went to a meeting together. They arrived a few minutes late; Sean was there and saw them come in. After the meeting, Sean walked up to her.

"Ya' didn't call this mornin,' Lassie," Sean said briskly.

Meg replied flippantly, "Well, didn't you read today's letter?"

"That's not the point. Meet me at the coffee shop tomorrow, noon sharp."

Meg sat with Warren and avoided Sean for the rest of the evening. After the meeting, Warren drove her home. When they pulled up to her apartment, they kissed passionately.

"Are you coming in tonight, Darling?"

"Not tonight," Warren said without emotion.

She started to protest and decided not to. Instead, she got out of the car and waved to him as he drove off, totally self-absorbed in her fantasy.

Warren went to the Jai Lai Lounge near Meg's apartment. He sat alone at the bar. He looked at the bottles behind the bar as the bartender walked over to him.

"So what'll it be?" the bartender asked.

Warren paused and struggled with his answer, "I'll have a..." He stopped, then said, "Give me an iced tea."

The bartender laughed, "Iced tea's at the restaurant around the corner, Bud. This is a bar if you didn't notice." He studied Warren, then said, "And you look like you need something stronger that iced tea."

Warren shrugged and forced a laugh.

"Yeah, you're right. Give me a double shot of Jack, straight up."

The bartender poured the double shot of whiskey. Warren downed it and motioned for a refill. The bartender refilled his glass.

Warren's face relaxed after he downed the second one.

After Meg made her 7 a.m. call to Sean the next morning, she called Warren. The phone rang and he did not answer. When his answering machine came on she said, "Are you there, Darling? Where could you be this early in the morning? Okay, I'll talk to you later, then."

She hung up the phone and headed out the door to work. She had taken a half day teaching assignment so that she could keep her appointment with Sean at noon.

When she got to the coffee shop, she headed for "their booth" toward the back. She ordered her Diet Pepsi and his hot tea. Sean arrived a few minutes later. They ordered lunch and shared light conversation as they ate. When they finished, Sean pushed back his plate, poured some hot tea, added five sugars, stirred the tea briskly, and fired up a cigarette.

"Here's how it is, Lassie. I want ya' ta' call me every mornin' at 7 a.m. sharp. No exceptions," he began emphatically.

"No matter how long a history ya' have with Warren, you're both babies in AA, teeterin' on the edge of a cliff. Nothin' and no one can get in the way of ya' bein' sober, Meg. And I won't open any more of your letters. From now on, you're goin' ta' have ta' tell me what's goin' on with ya.'"

Meg swallowed with difficulty; finally she said quietly, "It's just not that easy for me to talk to anyone."

"This is not a debate, Meg. This is serious. Ya' must be talkin' to me," Sean said. He stopped and took a breath.

"When's your meetin' with the FBI?"

Meg dropped her head, "Day after tomorrow."

"Call me in the mornin' at 7 a.m., and call me as soon as you're done meetin' with the FBI. Got it?"

Meg nodded yes, she knew it was pointless to protest.

Meg called Sean at 7 a.m. before she left for her FBI appointment; he gave her encouragement and support.

"Just tell the truth and everything will work out. I promise," he said confidently.

At 3 p.m., Meg stood outside the John W. Bricker Federal Building on North High Street that housed the local FBI office. She looked up at the massive structure; she never imagined her life taking her to this place, a place where one would expect to find hardened criminals. She went inside and found the FBI office where a federal agent greeted her. She had seen this man before; he was the one she noticed luring in the shadows over the past several months.

"I'm Agent Jim Richards and I'll be conducting our interview today," he said, emotionless, as he guided her into a tiny examining room with a table and two wooden chairs on either side. There was a light that hung over the table.

He was in plain clothes and had a badge attached to his belt. He carried a note pad. Meg had made every effort to dress conservatively in a plain black suit with a white blouse. She wore a multicolored blue scarf that showed under her jacket.

Richards motioned for Meg to sit down. Her mouth was dry and her stomach was churning. She was having trouble breathing.

"Ms. O'Neil, just so we are clear, this is about your bankruptcy that resulted from your renting Cobo Hall and doing..." he looks at his notes, "a three day party for Super Bowl weekend, known as the 'Biggest Game in Town for the Biggest Game in Town.'"

It sounded so sinister when he said it, she thought.

"Is that correct?" he continued, looking up from his notes.

Meg nodded.

"I need an audible response."

Meg whispered, "Yes."

"We have reason to believe that you have committed bankruptcy fraud which is a federal offense. It's been reported that you have a million dollars worth of hidden assets."

"Officer, all the assets I have in the world, I'm wearing," she said, her voice shaking.

Richards did not smile. He read aloud from his report. It listed many items it was believed Meg had hidden.

Much of it was a blur to Meg until she heard him say, "...and a classic antique, solid brass, Trapeze bed, that was to be willed to the Smithsonian Institute..."

Meg interrupted him and said defensively, "Sir, I bought that bed at a furniture store next to an X-rated theater on Woodward Avenue in Detroit. It wasn't made of brass, and it wasn't an antique. It ended up in my living room because it would not fit in my bedroom. It was quite a conversation piece. But I never thought I would be discussing it with the FBI!"

Richards looked her squarely in the eyes and said sternly, with no emotion, "Lady, it's been the talk of the bureau."

Meg's heart sank, dread overtook her. The interview lasted more than three hours, and she was consumed with a sense of doom as time dragged on. When it finally ended and she got back outside, it was raining. She shook her fist at God and said, "God, end this, now!"

Meg did not call Sean and did not go home. She drove around for hours. When she did get home, she tried to call Warren, but he didn't answer.

It was 1 a.m. and she was pacing the floor when the phone rang. It was Warren; he was drunk. Meg ran out the door to go save him. When she got to Warren's apartment, she burst in. She saw a bottle of Jack Daniels on the kitchen table. She paused and looked at the bottle. Then she saw Warren in a chair with a shotgun across his lap.

"You're finally here, bitch," he slurred.
He grabbed the bottle and guzzled some down, spilling it on his silk, designer shirt. Meg was horrified. How many times had they been together drunk like this?
She moved slowly toward Warren and the gun.

"Warren, give me the gun," she said with controlled panic.

Warren dropped his head. She seized the moment to grab the gun, he reacted and struggled with her for it. His finger was on the trigger; the gun was pointed at Meg. They struggled, and the shotgun went off.

Meg ran outside the apartment, put the gun in the trunk of her car, jumped in, and drove to the nearest pay phone. She got out and called Sean. When he answered he was groggy, she was sobbing.

"Sean, I need you."

"Where are ya,' Meg?" he said, as he pulled on his jeans. He grabbed a note pad and wrote down the address.

"Now listen to me," he said in a clear, decisive tone, "hold that phone in your hand until I get there.
Do you understand?"

He grabbed his coat and made a quick call before rushing out the door.

Sean's car screeched to a stop in front of the phone booth where Meg stood with her hand frozen to the receiver. Her face was red and blotchy from crying.

"Are ya' all right?" he said as he got out of his car. Meg nodded yes, dropped the phone, and ran to Sean, collapsing in his arms.

"Warren called. I went to him. He was drunk, very drunk. He had a shotgun..." she said, her voice trembling.

Abbey pulled up as Meg was speaking. Sean nodded to Abbey and she stood behind Meg, listening.

"We struggled." She looked at Sean with terror in her eyes. "Oh God, Oh God, it was pointed at me. It went off."

Abbey put her arms around Meg to steady her.

"Where's the gun?" Sean asked.

Meg's eyes were filled with terror, "In the trunk of my car."

"Where's Warren?"

"His place."

Sean showed controlled calm, "The address, Meg."

"420 Coventry."

Sean grabbed Meg's car keys.

"You're goin' home with Abbey. We'll sort this out tomorrow."

Sean walked back to Meg's car as she left with Abbey.

Abbey's home was warm and cozy. They sat in the kitchen, Scottish music played softly in the background. The soft light in the room came from the candle on the table. Abbey was fixing some Constant Comment tea. It was past 3 a.m., and Meg's sobs had subsided.

"I don't understand how this happened," Meg said.

Abbey stopped what she was doing, went to the table, sat next to Meg, and put her arm around her shoulder.

"Sean will handle it," Abbey said.

Meg was too tired to speak. She put her head down on the table and listened to the soft tones of the Scottish flute.

The next evening, Sean directed Meg to meet at his apartment. This was the first time she had been to his place. She got out of her car, went to the door, and rang the bell. Sean opened the door and welcomed her inside. She sat down on the sofa; she still looked exhausted and near tears. He brought her a Diet Pepsi and a KitKat bar. He got his hot tea and a KitKat bar and joined her on the sofa.

He was kind, but firm.

"Why didn't ya' call me when ya' finished with the FBI?"

"I don't know, Sean, I couldn't think straight," she said. "What if they put me in jail?"

"We'll cross that bridge when we come to it, Lassie. Right now, I want ya' ta' hear me."

Sean fired up a cigarette and took a long, deep drag. He looked into her eyes.

"Ya' never, never go on a 12th Step call alone. Never. No matter how well ya' think ya' know the person. Ya' can't keep anyone else sober, Lassie. It's only by the grace a' God that someone wasn't killed last night."

He took a drag off his cigarette.

"Warren'll pull ya' down into that black hole he's in 'cause you're barely sober yourself, Meg. Ya' have ta' let him go while he's drinkin.'"

Meg's head was down. She could not speak to acknowledge Sean's words.

The next morning, when Meg's alarm went off, she opened her eyes and said, "Please God, keep me sober today." She got out of bed and got down on her knees and prayed.

Meg met Sean at meetings every day. Sometimes they would meet at noon and then again for an evening meeting. She was beginning to feel connected.

At the end of every meeting, everyone would join hands and say the "Our Father" prayer. Instead of saying, "Forgive us our trespasses, as we forgive those who trespass against us," she would say, "Forgive us our sins, as we forgive those who sin against us." This was causing some commotion in the meetings as it caused a break in the group's rhythm during the prayer.

One of the members, Dave, went to Sean after a meeting, very agitated.

"You've got to do something about Meg saying 'sins.' It's messing everyone up. Make her say 'trespasses' like the rest of us," he told Sean.

"I'll take care of it. But let me handle it. Meg's real fragile right now."

Dave nodded.

Several days later, Sean invited Meg on a picnic and drove her to an area by the Olentangy River. It was a glorious early spring day. He spread a plaid blanket down for them to sit on. He had brought a bag of hamburgers, fries, an iced tea with five sugars for himself, and a Diet Pepsi for Meg. She seemed much more relaxed. She wore a button down shirt and jeans like Sean. They watched ducks and geese walk by, quacking loudly. Nearby, a group of pigeons milled around. Sean fired up a cigarette.

"Ya' know why we call newcomers pigeons?" Sean asked.

"Not really."

"Well, just watch 'em a minute."

They both watched the pigeons for a few moments. The pigeons walked around in circles, aimlessly.

"See 'em wanderin' around, not knowin' which way ta' go? That's what we're all like when we get ta' Alcoholics Anonymous. Ya' need alota instruction in the beginnin.' I reckon that you're Pigeon Number 847."

"Pigeon 847?" Meg laughed.

"Yep!" Sean tried to be casual, "And you're about ta' get some instructions. Ya' know when we say the 'Our Father' prayer? You've been sayin' sins instead of trespasses. It's throwin' everybody off, so ya' gotta start sayin' trespasses."

Meg went berserk.

"Bullshit," she screamed, "trespassing is going onto someone's property when there's a sign in the yard saying not to. Sins are what got me to the program. I'm right and the rest of you are wrong."

Sean lost his temper.

"Damn it ta' hell, Meg. You'd rather be right than happy; this is not a debate. From now on, you're ta' say trespasses in the prayer."

Meg was furious, she glared at him, "I will not. You have no right to tell me how to pray. It's a God of my understanding, remember."

Sean pulled back, regained control. He fired up another cigarette and thought a moment.

"We could negotiate."

Meg waited for him to continue, controlling her anger.

Sean spoke slowly and deliberately.

"If ya' say trespasses instead a' sins, ya' can ask for jelly bread instead of daily bread."

Meg paused and calmed down a bit. She gave this solution some thought before she spoke.

"I'll think about it."

Later that night, Sean was on an official date with Darlene, the attractive, dark haired girl he'd been talking to at meetings. Sean was wearing his blue ruffled shirt with his neatly pressed jeans. A photographer came up to the table. Sean put his arm around her and beamed into the camera. The flash was blinding.

Meg attended her first all women's meeting with Abbey. Meg wore a conspicuous button that said: Hopelessly Hetero. Some of the women at the meeting rolled their eyes at Meg. At the end of the meeting, when they said the "Our Father," Meg said: *Give us this day our jelly bread, and forgive us our trespasses as we forgive those who trespass against us.*

Meg and Abbey walked out of the meeting.

"Did you say 'jelly bread?'" Abbey said.

"Don't even ask," Meg said indignantly.

The next morning, Meg was on the phone with Sean complaining about the women's meeting.

"I just hated that stupid women's meeting," she told him, "they all looked at me funny."

"Try goin' without the button," he replied.

"Who told you?"

"I'm your sponsor, Meg. I know everything."

Meg was silent.

"I'm goin' ta' have ta' go outa town tonight for business. I want ya' ta' stay close to Abbey. Just don't drink an' go ta' meetin's and I'll call ya' when I get back."

It was the first time since Sean had become her sponsor that Meg did not hear his voice at 7 a.m. She did not sleep for several days and it was difficult to function. She did not go to meetings, and she did not call Abbey. By the fourth day, she needed to sleep and a friend at work offered her a sleeping pill. She wrapped it in a napkin and put it in her pocket. That night, she took the pill out of her pocket and set it on the counter. Maybe she wouldn't take it. But she needed to sleep and it wasn't alcohol, she thought. She was anxious. She paced around her apartment. Finally, she went to the counter, picked up the pill, popped it in her mouth, and swallowed it. The next morning, Meg slept through her alarm.

Sean's business trip was grueling. The days were long and he could not get to meetings or even call his own sponsor. By the fourth day, he was in his fourth hotel. It was early evening when he went got to his hotel room. He threw his suitcase down on the bed. He plopped down in a chair, exhausted. He sat there for a few minutes and fired up a cigarette. Sean looked around the room, and his eyes fixated on the wet bar. He got up and went to the bar. He picked up a bottle of

Scotch whiskey; he held it in his hands and really looked it over. He put it down and went back to the chair and sat down. He took a drag off his cigarette, picked up the phone, and called Meg. It rang.

Meg was still in bed when the phone rang. She reached for the phone and nearly dropped it when she answered.

"Hello."

"Howdy Meg," Sean said, trying to sound cheerful and upbeat, "How ya' doin,' Little Missy?"

Meg recognized Sean's voice, but had difficulty responding. "This is Meg," she slurred.

"I know, Lassie, I called you." Sean immediately sized up the situation. "How was work today?" he continued.

"Okay," Meg lied.

"Well, what're ya' doin?"

"Nothing."

"Ya' goin' ta' a meetin' tonight?"

"Sure," Meg lied again.

"What's wrong, Meg? Ya' sound strange."

"Oh, I was just sleeping."

"At six in the evening?"

Meg was a little more alert.

"Yeah. I hadn't slept since you left town, so a friend of mine at work gave me one of her sleeping pills..."

Sean cut her off. He was furious, he fired up another cigarette as he talked.

"Jesus H. Christ! Ya' took a mood alterin' drug. No one ever died from lack of sleep. And ya' lied before, didn't ya'? Ya' didn't even go ta' work ta' day."

Meg was defensive. "What's the big deal. It wasn't alcohol or cocaine. It was just one little sleeping pill."

"JUST a sleepin' pill. Why'd ya' take it? Your intent was ta' alter your mood. That's a direct violation of your sobriety. I've known a lota people who just took a sleepin' pill or a Librium or a Valium, and they eventually went back ta' drinkin' and druggin' and died of this fuckin' disease. It's cunning, bafflin,' powerful, and very patient. Ya' gotta change your sobriety date."

Meg was fully awake.

"Change my date? Give up my two years of sobriety and start back at day one? I WILL NOT!" she screamed.

Sean spoke with great emotion, "Ya' don't have two years of sobriety, Meg. You're dry, not sober. If ya' don't change your sobriety date, every time ya' say 'I've been sober since March 10, 1981,' a little voice will go off in your head that says, 'except for the time ya' used that sleepin' pill' and that voice will get so loud that it will finally kill ya.' It's about gettin' honest, Lassie. And your sobriety date is the only thing you'll ever have that is 100% bonafide honest."

"But..."

"No discussion," Sean continued, "this is non-negotiable. Change your sobriety date or get a new sponsor. I won't watch ya' die."

"Fuck you!" Meg shrieked as she slammed down the receiver in Sean's ear.

Sean slowly put the receiver back on the cradle, he took a long drag off his cigarette and smiled just a little.

Meg got up earlier than usual. She went to work and thought about Sean all day. She decided to go to the Wednesday West Fifth discussion meeting and discuss her dilemma. She explained, "I took one little sleeping pill. It wasn't alcohol or cocaine. So I'd like to know if I really need to change my sobriety date."

Meg heard the full array of comments as it went around the room:

A clear eyed, well dressed woman said, "For me, my sobriety date represents my being completely free of all mood altering chemicals and that means anything that affects me from the neck up. I would have to change it, if it were me, Meg."

A large, burly man, blue-collar type said, "I'm a lyin' cheatin' SOB, but when I say I've been sober since January 4, 1970, it's the God's truth and I'm not willing to compromise. It's His Grace keeps me sober."

A wretched looking woman with droopy eyes said, "I take cough syrup with alcohol in it when I have a cold, and I use NyQuil to sleep at night and I haven't changed my sobriety date."

Sean entered the door at the back of the room and fired up a cigarette. Meg had her back to the door so she did not see him.

The man sitting to the right of Meg was handsome and well-dressed. He looked like a successful businessman or a college professor.

"I'm John and I'm an alcoholic," he said.

"Hi John," everyone said in unison.

"Hi everyone. You know, Meg, I've been coming around these rooms for almost ten years now. When I was three years sober, I had a home, a wife, two great kids, a very successful business, and one day, I was real nervous, so I took one little Valium. Who would know? A few weeks later I drank a couple a beers. Who would know? And a few weeks after that I was downing a bottle of Wild Turkey and the race was on. I drank and drugged for a year and a half. Long enough to lose my home, my family, my business, and when I crawled back into these rooms, I was barely alive," he looked Meg in the eyes, "so don't change your date today--because you will."

Meg was stunned by his words, a cold chill went down her spine.

Sean saw her face and was relieved.

After the meeting, Sean and Meg left together. He put his arm around her shoulder.

"I'm changing my sobriety date. It's June 7, 1983," she said quietly.

"I'm real proud of ya' Meg. You've just taken the very first step ta' bein' honest about your recovery."

Part Three

Sean straddled his Black Harley-Davidson Hog on that gorgeous early summer day. The sun glistened on the Olentangy River; there was not a cloud in the sky. He was wearing a black leather jacket, black leather pants, and boots. He was on a pay phone in the middle of a call to Meg.

"...so meet me here in 30 minutes," he said.

As soon as he hung up the phone, he raced off on his bike. The wind hit his face and his red hair blew in the wind. He pushed his new toy to it's limits. He rode into the park at full throttle to the spot where he had told Meg to meet him. He was polishing his bike when she drove up. Meg was wearing a flimsy, frilly, black cotton summer dress, white Keds tennis shoes, and no socks. She got out of her car and bounced up to Sean; she walked around Sean's bike, oohing and aahing at how beautiful it was. Sean proudly pointed out the special features one could only find on a Harley.

He climbed on the bike, revved up the engine, and beamed at her, "Hop on Meg! We're goin' ta' Ride the Wind!"

Meg stepped back, defiantly crossed her arms, and stomped her foot.

"I'm not getting on that bike without a helmet!"

Sean was taken back by her comment.

"Let me see if I understand ya,' Lassie," he said with disbelief, "Not one inch of your entire body is properly covered, but ya' want ta' protect the one thing that has screwed ya' up your entire life?"

"Yes I do!"

Moments later, Meg and Sean rode full speed down a beautiful, wooded country road near the park. Sean was loving every moment of it. Meg was holding on for dear life. The wind caught her dress and blew it up around her waist, exposing her bare legs and white Keds tennis shoes.

But, Meg was wearing a shiny black Harley Davidson helmet.

Sean and Meg met at meetings most days, they would share dinner, and they met at the park by the Olentangy to spend time reading the AA text book, referred to as the Big Book. The first 164 pages held the directions for the program of AA, and the second half of the book was filled with stories of recovery. Several months had passed since Meg had changed her sobriety date.

They walked along one of the well worn wooded paths and found a perfect spot under one of the magnificent shade trees. The sun cascaded through the trees as they sat down to talk.

"Sobriety seems a lot harder now that I'm being honest. Before I could hide, now everyone knows what a phony I am," Meg said.

"I know, Baby. All us al-keys are actors on the stage of life. But when we quit playin' God and let Him do the directin,' our lives change. It get's better. And we're the it."

Meg laughed just a little.

"Just remember, no matter what, I'm here for ya,' Lassie," Sean said.

They enjoyed the serenity of their surroundings. Meg looked at Sean for a long moment.

"Who are you, really, Sean Patrick MacIntosh?" she asked.

Sean was evasive, "Whatda ya' mean?"

"Don't answer with a question. Who are you? All I know about you is that you go to meetings and help people like me stay sober."

Sean looked off into the distance. Finally, he said.

"Isn't that enough? Ya' need ta' know more?"

"Yes, like what was your life like in Scotland? What was your family like? How did you end up here in Columbus, Ohio?"

Sean showed his uneasiness; he reached in his pocket, pulled out a cigarette, and fired it up. He was thoughtful before he spoke.

"Ma' Mom is a grand lady," he began with a soft tone that was out of character for him, "she still lives in Scotland along with my two older brothers. I miss seein' her, but we talk on the phone twice a month. Ma' Dad, he wasn't around much. He was a musician. He really loved his Scotch whiskey. He died when I was in high school. I got married young and moved ta' America for a *'better life.'* I had a great job on the East Coast. One day I got drunk, walked in and quit my job. My wife left me and took our baby girl with her. I headed for California and ran outta gas and money in Cincinnati, so that was where I stayed. And this is where God saw fit ta' lead me ta' the doors of Alcoholics Anonymous. M' job moved me to Columbus about a month before I met ya.'"

Meg started to reach her hand to Sean, wanting to give him support. She thought better of it and pulled back. She paused. After a time, she reached out and laid her hand on top of his. Sean leaned his head back against the tree, soaking up the sun. Then he took Meg's hand in his and firmly held it as they sat in silence.

Later that night, Sean sat alone on his sofa. He fired up a cigarette and took a long, slow drag. He pulled out his wallet. He removed an old, faded photo of a man holding a trumpet in one hand; his other hand was on the shoulder of a young boy. He lovingly replaced the photo into his wallet. He got up, grabbed his keys, and rushed out the door.

Sean rode his shiny, black Harley Davidson at full throttle down the highway. He turned off onto a side road still going much faster than he should have been. The moonlight and stars were brilliant. They shimmered off the black of his bike. The wind blew through his hair. He rode as fast as his bike would go.

After work the next day, Sean took Darlene to dinner and then they went back to his place to watch a John Wayne Western.

Sean was in bed with Darlene. They were making out hot and heavy. The clock on his nightstand said 11:35 p.m. when the phone rang.

"Howdy," he answered.

"It's Meg," her voice was barely audible.

Sean was serious, "What is it Meg?"

"I can't do it, Sean. I can't stay alive and sober for the rest of my life."

"I know Luv," he replied with kindness, "That's why ya' only have ta' do it for ta-day. Hold on a minute."

Sean got out of bed, put his hand over the receiver and said to Darlene, "I've gotta take this call."

She looked disgusted as he left the bedroom. Sean carried the phone into the kitchen, put on a pot of water, sat down at the table, and fired up a cigarette.

"So, let's talk about just stayin' sober and alive for today, and we'll do tomorrow when it comes."

"But that's the worst part, the mornings. When I open my eyes, the first thing I think is, oh my God, the FBI is after me and my leg hurts and I probably have some rare disease and I don't have health insurance and so why don't I drink but then that will take too long so why don't I just kill myself. And then, my life goes down from there," she cried.

Sean listened with understanding.

"Ya' know, we al-keys don't have time to change our thinkin.' We gotta change our actions first, our thinkin' will follow."

Meg was shaky and holding on to the phone for dear life. Sean made his cup of tea with his traditional five sugars. He fired up another cigarette.

"We've all got this little devil that sits on our shoulder and whispers that crazy thinkin' to us. It's called ODAP, our devilish al-key-holic personality"

Sean was animated; he loved AA, "Now here's the good news. There's a split second when we open our eyes in the mornin' before ODAP kicks in. As fast as our minds are, we can only hold one thought at a time. So, here's what I want ya' ta' do. When ya' open your eyes, shout: *God, I love ya,' you're terrific, you're doin' for me what I cannot do for myself.* And while you're sayin' it, get down on your knees and ask Him ta' keep ya' sober, just for that day."

Sean looked at his kitchen clock; it said 12:01 a.m.

"Well, Lassie, it's 12:01. Ya' made it through another day. Call me at 7 a.m."

When Sean returned to his bedroom, Darlene was sound asleep.

The next morning, she left with a basket of Sean's dirty laundry. He kissed her goodbye. Meg called as he was finishing his tea, and before he headed to work.

When Meg opened her eyes the same morning, she shouted, "God, I love you. You're terrific. You're doing for me what I cannot do for myself!"

While she was saying this, she got out of bed and dropped to her knees by the side of the bed.

Later that night, Darlene and Sean stood on his front porch. She had his laundry basket of clean, neatly folded clothes. She threw the basket down and some of the clothes spilled out. Sean stooped down to pick them up. She screamed at him and shook her finger in his face. He looked like a lost, defenseless puppy dog. She stormed off the porch, got in her car, and left. Sean looked bewildered as he watched her go.

Sean picked up the rest of the spilled clothes and carried his laundry basket inside. He dropped it on the floor in the living room. His coffee table was covered with KitKat wrappers and an overflowing ashtray. He plopped down on the sofa, fired up a cigarette, took a long drag, and looked baffled.

Several nights later, Sean was outside the AA meeting putting the moves on a cute young blond named Tammie. His face was animated as he talked to her. She was looking at Sean with googoo eyes and giggling. They went inside and sat down together. Meg came into the meeting a few minutes later and Sean motioned for her to come and sit with him. She obliged.

Meg still wanted to keep people at a distance, especially women. She still wanted to hide behind her written words. The more she resisted change the more painful her life seemed, and empty, very empty.

After the meeting, Sean told Meg he wanted to talk with her a minute. He said goodbye to Tammie, then walked outside with Meg.

What started as a civilized conversation quickly escalated into a screaming match. They stood toe to toe in the parking lot shouting at one another. Sean threw down his cigarette and ground it out with his boot. His face was bright red from yelling. Others leaving the meeting stayed as far away from the two of them as possible.

"You're three months sober and ya' don't even know what the First Step says!"

"I do too. I ADMITTED!" Meg screeched.

"NO, you're wrong!"

"I ADMITTED!" Meg was furious.

"NO!" Sean raged.

They continued to argue, oblivious to everyone else in the parking lot.

"It's sounds like they're gonna kill each other," a passerby said.

Sean continued, "Ya' don't know the First Step, Meg."

Tears of anger streamed down her face, she stomped her foot, her body was shaking.

"I HATE you. I do. I ADMITTED!" she billowed.

Sean put his hands on her shoulders and gently pushed her back. He looked into her eyes for a long moment, demanding her full attention.

Then, very quietly, "Luv, the first word of the First Step is 'We,' 'We admitted we were powerless over al-key-hol--that our lives had become unmanageable.' And if ya' don't get the first word of the First Step, you'll die of this fuckin' disease."

Meg fell into his arms, totally spent.

Sean asked Abbey and Robin to spend more time with Meg. The three of them got together at Abbey's on Saturday afternoon. They sat at the kitchen table, with a pile of small, smooth stones, permanent marking pens, and clear nail polish. They wrote sayings on the stones like: One Day At A Time, Easy Does It, The Kingdom Is Inside, First Things First, and The Program Works If You Work It.

"What are these again?" Meg asked.

"Recovery Rocks," Robin said.

"Recovery Rocks?" Meg said.

"Yep," Abbey said, "My first sponsor in Boulder taught me to make them. You carry some of them with you at all times, and when you see someone at a meeting who needs cheering up, you give him one. In the beginning, it was the only way I could pass on some recovery. Get it?"

Meg nodded.

"You're doing a great job, Meg," Robin complimented her writing on the stones.

"Thanks," Meg said, obviously pleased with herself.

After writing on the rocks and polishing them, they were set aside to dry.

"How long have you been sober?" Meg asked Abbey.

"It will be four years on April 16th. And I didn't think I could do this thing for four days when I got here. I lost my husband and son because of alcohol and drugs. We say, *There are no dues or fees for AA membership*, but I paid a mighty high price to get here. So did alot of other people," Abbey said, focused on writing on her recovery rock, "I came back to Columbus about a year ago and my parents have been helping me get back on my feet."

The hours passed by quickly and when Meg left she realized that she had really enjoyed herself with those two women. Meg went home and spent the evening alone, clearing out some of her boxes of paper. One particular box was overflowing. She threw away a few papers, looked at a few and put them back in the box. She picked up her journal and sat down.

She wrote: *I made recovery rocks today and I have no clue how that is going to keep me sober.*

Sean had a date with Tammie and they ended up at his place. They were in bed and Sean was leaning against the pillow, smoking a cigarette. Tammie leaned her head on his arm, animated as she talked. Sean took a drag off his cigarette. He was daydreaming, not hearing a word she was saying.

Sean was sharing his story at the Friday Night Speakers Meeting at the Oak Street Club in Cincinnati, Ohio. Meg and Abbey went with him for the road trip from Columbus. In fact, Abbey's dad loaned them his Mercedes Benz. Sean was thrilled. He was driving, Abbey was in the passenger seat, and Meg was in the back. He was speeding down I-71. They were all happy and laughing and singing at the top of their lungs. A cigarette dangled from Sean's mouth.

"It was mighty nice of your Dad to let us use his car, Abbey," he said.

He channel surfed and stopped at a station playing the Beatles tune, "Let It Be." He flipped his cigarette out the window with great flair. They all sang along with the radio.

"Ya' know girls, it doesn't get any better than this. Driving down the highway in a Mercedes Benz, sober," Sean quipped.

Janis Joplin came on the radio singing, "Oh Lord, won't ya' buy me Mercedes Benz." Sean sang along. He held the steering wheel with his right hand, reached inside his jacket with his left hand and pulled out a 357 Magnum. He put his arm out the open window and fired the gun in the air several times. Meg laughed and applauded. Abbey freaked out.

"Are you crazy?" Abbey screamed, out of control.

Sean was calm and deliberate.

"Nope, just always wanted ta' drive a Mercedes down the highway and fire a gun at the same time."

"But you're going to hit something," Abbey gasped.

"No I'm not, Lassie. Just relax. I'm shootin' it up in the air."

"Well, the bullets have to come down sometime," Abbey said with disgust, "You are totally insane."

Sean and Meg were puzzled by Abbey's over-reaction.

Sean put the gun away. He and Meg continued singing and bouncing along with the tunes on the radio. Abbey was bent over in the front passenger seat with her hand on her forehead. She shook her head in disbelief.

They arrived safely at the meeting. The room was full of new faces. Meg and Abbey sat in the front row, listening attentively.

Sean was energized.

"I didn't get sober ta' be miserable. The God of my understandin' wants me ta' be happy, ta' laugh and have fun and enjoy my time on this earth."

He paused.

"I picture God sittin' up in Heaven at a giant control panel with little television screens. He can just zoom in on us from time to time. He'll adjust one of the knobs and see what I'm doin' and say: *There goes Sean screwin' up again.* But the miracle is, He loves me anyway. And he must have a fantastic sense of humor 'cause He made us Al-kies."

Sean paused again and was thoughtful and emotional as he continued.

"What if when we die, the only thing God says to us is: *Did you enjoy being on earth?* And some of us might whine and say: *Oh, I didn't have enough of this or that.* And God says: *No, did ya' enjoy being on earth? Did ya' see my rainbows and sunrises and sunsets and flowers. Were ya' kind and lovin' to those around ya?'*
'Cause if ya' enjoyed earth, you'll fit right in here in Heaven, and if ya' didn't, well, there's just no room for ya' here. I wanna say to Him: *Oh yes, Father, I loved every minute of it.*"

After the meeting, about thirty people met at a local dance hall. They whooped it up, dancing and laughing. The entire crowd conspicuously drinking sodas. Sean had an iced tea.

Several days later, Meg was at one of her regular weekly meetings. Sean had explained that she needed a home group where she helped set up the meeting and was there every week so people got to know her. Also, there were meetings that she would attend most of the time. People milled around before the meeting, greeting one another and talking. Meg noticed a woman who was standing off to the side. She looked lost. She was wearing a semiformal dress and scuffed high heels. Meg knew the look; she was a newcomer. Meg reached in her pocket and pulled out a Recovery Rock. She looked at it thoughtfully for a moment, then stepped up to her.

"Hi, I'm Meg. Glad you're here."

"I'm Karen."

Meg smiled as she put the Recovery Rock in Karen's hand. Karen looked at her with distrust. Meg asked her how long she had been coming to meetings and Karen said it was her first time. Meg then gave her a card.

"Here's my phone number," Meg said, "if you have any questions or you ever need to talk, just give me a call."

Meg realized she was actually calling Abbey and Robin occasionally. She always called Sean at 7 a.m. But that morning, she had been up for hours. She was anxious, she looked at herself in the mirror, she picked up the phone, then put it down. Tears filled her eyes. She looked in the mirror again and studied her face. It was 6 a.m. when she finally dialed Sean's number. It rang loudly. Sean picked up the phone and was groggy and disoriented.

"Hello," he said, then he started coughing.

"It's Meg, it's important," her voice was almost inaudible.

Sean forced alertness, he fired up a cigarette.

"Are ya' okay, Baby? Are ya' sober?"

"Yes, I'm sober."

She began to sob.

"What is it, Meg?" he said tenderly.

"I've got to ask you something important, and you have to promise to tell the truth."

"It better be important, Lassie. It's 6 a.m."

"Promise?"

"Promise what?"

"To tell the truth."

Sean was frustrated, "I promise."

Meg took a deep breath, "Do you think I'm pretty?"

"Damn it ta' hell. Ya' called me at 6 in the mornin' ta' ask me if you're pretty?"

"Just tell the truth," Meg said, crying loudly.

Sean was silent for a long moment.

"Yes, Lassie. I think you're pretty, very pretty," he said gently, "why are ya' askin?'"

"Because I looked in the mirror this morning when I woke up and I thought I was pretty for the first time in my life. And I had to be sure."

Meg choked on her tears.

"You're very pretty, Meg," he paused, "Now don't call me again before 7 a.m. or I'll break your face."

Meg laughed through her tears.

"Call me later," Sean said as he tenderly put the receiver back on the phone.

Meg was sending out resumes and rushed into the post office to mail them. She bumped into Warren. It was the first time she had seen him in almost a year when she struggled with him for the gun. They both showed shock at this unexpected encounter. She reached in her pocket and pulled out a Recovery Rock. She put it in his hand, held it for a moment, looked at him lovingly but did not speak. Warren was frozen as he looked back at Meg. After she walked away, he looked at the rock.

It said: *The Program Works If You Work It.*

Sean was determined to show Meg how to have fun in sobriety. He planned a potluck party at Abbey's parents' home with the help of Abbey and Robin. A banner hung across the back of the house that said, **First Annual Pigeon Potluck.** More than fifty people milled around the huge back yard that sunny Saturday afternoon in June. They were dressed in fun, colorful, casual clothes. Some were already in their bathing suits. Sean, Abbey, Robin, and Meg greeted and directed people. Karen came and looked particularly lost in the crowd. More and more people arrived with covered dishes and homemade desserts. The food was placed on a long row of tables set up on one side of the yard. Two grills were going with hot dogs and hamburgers. Everyone was welcome, recovering people and their families, spouses, children, and friends. There were picnic tables and round aluminum umbrella tables, sprinkled around the yard. People were enjoying the swimming pool in one area of the yard. In another area, there was a luxurious outdoor patio that was being used as a dance floor. Music blasted; people danced.

Sean was walking around in shorts, shades, with a cigarette in one hand and an iced tea in the other. Tammie followed behind him like a puppy dog.

Everyone was laughing and happy and having a wonderful time sober. Sean walked over to a stage area near the dance floor and picked up a microphone. He checked to see if the sound was on and caused it to screech.

Sean commanded attention from the crowd.

"Hell-ooo everybody! Glad you could come and share in the festivities of the First Annual Pigeon Potluck party. First, I want to thank Abbey and her parents for providing this wonderful place for our party."

Everyone applauded.

"And now, I want to introduce someone we all know and love, my Pigeon Number 847, who will present the first weenie."

There was thunderous applause as Meg went to the stage area carrying a silver platter with a lone hot dog on it. She held it so that everyone could see it. Meg was beaming. Sean took the hot dog off the plate, and with great showmanship, took a bite of it.

He laughed, "It's ooo-kay!" He held up what was left of the hot dog and said, "And remember guys, as long as your weenie is okay, everything else will work out just fine. This party has officially begun."

Karen attempted to relax. She looked for Meg in the crowd. When she found her, she said, "Can we talk later?"

"We can talk right now," Meg replied.

Meg led Karen to a quieter spot in the yard. Meg's eyes were bright and shining as she looked at Karen, distrust and fear showed in Karen's face.

"So, what can I do for you?"

"I don't understand how this thing works, but everyone talks about a sponsor, so will you be my sponsor," she blurted out.

"I would be honored to be your sponsor," Meg said, surprised and touched, "that would make you my Pigeon Number

One. Sean is your Grand Sponsor, so he can help us learn together. Would that be okay with you?"

Karen nodded yes.

"Are you willing to take directions, even when you don't understand them or believe they will help you?

Karen agreed.

"I promise I will never ask you to do anything I have not done myself. And the first thing I want you to do is call me every morning at 7:30 a.m. sharp. Okay?

Karen nodded yes and smiled.

Meg grabbed her hand, "Now let's party!"

They rejoined the festivities. Sean returned to the stage area and picked up the microphone.

"Could I have your attention, please? Quiet. I need your attention for a very special announcement."

He waited for everyone to quiet down. There was a medallion his hand.

"Stayin' sober is a one day at a time deal. But the days do add up. So, I am very proud to give this one year medallion to a very special young lady, my pigeon number 847, Meg!"

Meg went to the stage to the uproarious applause of everyone there. Sean put the medallion in her hand and gave her a hug. Meg looked at it and beamed.

Part Four

It was a bright Monday afternoon in late September. Meg pulled up in front of her apartment, got out of her car, picked up her mail, and went inside. She was dressed in a clean, pressed white blouse, a sky blue skirt and jacket, and low heels. Her make-up was moderate, a natural beauty look. Her attractive appearance reflected her recovery. She threw the mail down on the table and changed into jeans and a T-shirt.

As she walked back into the living room, there was a knock at the door. It was a postman with a registered letter for her. She signed for it and looked at it as she closed the door. She began to shake, terror filled her face. She tore open the letter, glanced at it, and
grabbed the phone.

"Hell-o," Sean said cheerfully.

There was silence.

"I said, 'hell-o,'" he said again.

Meg was gasping for air.

"Oh my God. I just got a registered letter from the Federal Grand Jury in Detroit. They are going to bring a federal indictment against me. Sean, I'm looking at one to five years in Federal Prison," Meg sobbed.

She clutched the letter to her chest, crumpling it, and dissolved into a chair. The letter fell to the floor as she held on to the phone with one and held her head in the other.

Sean struggled to grasp what was going on. He was shaking as he fired up a cigarette.

"Baby, Baby, calm down, what indictment, what's this about?"

"The FBI thing. The 'hidden funds.' Remember?"

"I thought that was all behind ya' Luv."

"Well, it's not; it just blew up in my face. They want a whole lotta money that I don't have, or I'll have to go to jail," Meg sobbed, out of control.

"Meg, listen to me," he said, trying to get her attention, "Meg, listen. It'll be all right. I promise. We'll pay them back the money. I'll help ya.' How much do ya' owe 'em?"

Meg caught her breath and said clearly, "Two hundred and fifty-six thousand dollars."

Without missing a beat, Sean said, "Then on the other hand, we really don't know God's will for ya.' Perhaps it is ta' do one to five Federal."

Meg wailed loudly.

"I'll be by for ya' in twenty minutes. We're goin' ta' a meetin,'" he continued.

Sean picked her up for a meeting and over the next weeks, they attended more meetings than usual. He took her out to dinner at his favorite restaurant, The Claremont. He would have his usual shrimp cocktail, steak, and baked potato. He would order her the same and while he enjoyed his meal, she would just look at her plate. Meg had seen several attorneys and when they reviewed the details of her case, they had handed her back her file and refused to take her case. The stress was showing, she was haggard and unkempt.

Sean and Abbey stood by his car before the noon meeting. Meg had not yet arrived.

"Abbey, it doesn't look good. Meg's had two attorneys refuse ta' take her case. I'm afraid she's goin' ta' do prison time."

"No matter what, you can't let her know you're worried. You're her strength. You've got to keep her believing this will all work out."

Sean nodded his agreement.

"I'll be callin' ya' Luv," he said as Meg drove up.

The weeks of discouragement since finding out about the Federal Grand Jury Indictment had left Meg bedraggled. She sat in the meeting numb and expressionless.

The chairman, Bob, asked if anyone was attending his first AA meeting. A woman in her fifties stood up.

"I'm Wendy. I'm a school teacher and I was drunk all weekend and I didn't feed my cat and I just can't live like this anymore."

Meg flew into an instant rage, jumped out of her seat, lunged toward the woman, screaming, "I'm going to kill you, Bitch!"

Older members gasped as Sean grabbed Meg and dragged her outside of the meeting room.

"What are ya' doin' Meg? Calm down."

"But Sean, that woman hasn't hit bottom. She doesn't know what pain is. I'm facing the Federal Grand Jury; she didn't feed her damn cat!"

Sean restrained her.

"Oh Lassie," he said softly, "everybody's bottom is different. Ya' mus'n't scare people like that."

Meg's jaws were clenched, "Well, can I at least kick her in the shins?"

"No," Sean said emphatically.

Meg looked into his eyes, burst into tears, and fell into his arms, exhausted. He comforted her and rocked her until she calmed down and could return to the meeting.

Afterwards, Meg was walking toward her car when a man from the meeting came up to her. She had not met him before.

"Hi Meg, I'm Michael. I don't really know you, but I've been praying for you with what you are going through. I have the name of an attorney who may be able to help you," he said, handing her a slip of paper with a name and phone number.

Meg took the paper and acknowledged him but did not speak. Later that day, she made the call to the attorney and several days later she kept an appointment with her.

"Hello Margaret, I'm Jillian Reed. Please sit down and tell me what brings you to my office today," Jillian said.

They shook hands. Meg sat down and Jillian poured her a glass of water. Meg handed Jillian the letter from the Federal Grand Jury. Jillian quickly read it.

"Why don't you tell me what happened in your own words."

Meg cleared her throat and took a sip of water.

"It's not very pretty, but here goes. I stopped drinking and drugging in March of '81 and when I came out of the fog, I thought I needed to do something to recoup what I'd lost financially. Well, one of my last big drunks was Super Bowl weekend in New Orleans in January of '81. And I realized that the Super Bowl was going to be in Detroit in 1982. And I thought, hey, why don't I throw a party. I went to Cobo Hall in Downtown Detroit and met the director and told him my idea and he thought it was a great idea, too. So, I said, I'm here to rent 400,000 square foot of Cobo Hall to throw this party. Would you draw the contract so I can secure the venue? And he said sure and he did and we both signed it and he didn't ask me if I had the money to pay for it."

Jillian's face showed total disbelief and amazement.

"How were you able to get in to see the director?" she asked.

Meg laughed a little, "Oh that was easy. I just showed up at his office and said to his secretary, 'would you tell John Banning that Margaret Megan O'Neil is here to see him?' and about twenty minutes later I was meeting with him. That's what I'd do when I wanted to meet with someone who had no real reason to meet with me--just show up--and it usually worked."

Jillian shook her head, "Go on."

"Well, pretty much from April to the following January, I put the party together. I wasn't drinking, but I wasn't doing very well either. I'd force myself to dress up and go out the door and meet with people. I'd come home and lock myself in and just hold on mostly. Anyway, the party was called The Biggest Game in Town for the Biggest Game in Town and I was nicknamed Super Bowl Momma in all the press articles. The teams that year were the Cincinnati Bengals and the San Francisco 49ers. I'd advertised and made alot of contacts in those two cities as well as in Detroit. I expected to break even and maybe make enough to live on for a year and do one of these parties for every Super Bowl after that. What happened was the weather."

Meg took a sip of water, "It was about the worst weather in the history of Detroit and most of the country and the people I expected from San Francisco and Cincinnati didn't even get into town until Sunday. The weather was so bad that the freeways to Downtown Detroit were closed. So, no one came to the party."

The attorney was absolutely speechless.

Meg rattled on, "After that, it was time to pay the bills and there wasn't any money. I went to all the creditors and told them there wasn't any money and I had to file bankruptcy. I came back here to start over. Then, the FBI started investigating me because someone said I had 'hidden assets,' which I don't and that no one in their right mind would do such a thing. You know, rent Cobo Hall with no money. So, I went to AA because I wanted to kill myself and I didn't know what else to do. And I've been going ever since."

Meg pulled out another piece of paper and handed it to Jillian.

"Here is a list of respectable people I've gotten to know who said that they would be character witnesses for me. One is even a state supreme court justice. So, do you think you can keep me out of prison?"

Jillian leaned back in her chair and caught her breath. Her expression showed that she was blown away by what she had just heard. She took a few moments to regain her professional decorum. She chose her words carefully.

"Meg, they are charging you with bankruptcy fraud and that's a felony. However, if what you have told me is true, you are not guilty of this felony. But you are guilty of grandiosity, big time. Luckily, grandiosity is not a felony. I know a little bit about the 12-step program you are attending. It has helped several people I care about. Now, let me tell you who I am. I'm married to an FBI agent. Before I became a criminal defense attorney, I was a prosecutor for the Federal Grand Jury and I wrote the law they are using against you."

Meg did not grasp the importance of Jillian's words.

"Does this mean you'll take my case?"

"For now, I want to make a few calls on your behalf. Keep going to your meetings and don't drink. I'll call you in a few days."

Jillian stood up, ending the meeting. She walked around her desk, shook Meg's hand, and led her to the door.

When Meg got outside, she looked up and sighed, "Thank you God!"

That night, after the meeting, Sean and Meg met at the coffee shop. They sat in their favorite booth. Sean had his hot tea with five sugars. He fired up a cigarette as he listened to Meg.

"I guess she's taking my case because she said she'd make some calls and get back to me." Meg was talking so fast that she was barely taking a breath. "But she said she was married to an FBI agent. Why would she tell me that unless she had heard about the trapeze bed? Maybe she isn't going to take my case." She paused and remembered, "Oh yeah, and she said don't drink and go to meetings."

The following Saturday, Sean told Meg he had a surprise for her and he would pick her up at noon. They pulled into a boat yard filled with recreational crafts in various conditions. It was a sunny, cool afternoon and they were both wearing jackets.

"So, this is your big surprise, a boat yard in September?"

"I bought me one."

"But you can't use it now."

"I know, Lassie, but I just love a good bargain. I thought we could spend a few hours cleanin' it up so it'll be ready for the spring."

When they pulled up to Sean's boat, Meg rolled her eyes. His boat was a disaster. After they unloaded all of the cleaning supplies, Meg filled a bucket with soapy water, put on rubber gloves, and used a heavy duty scrub brush to clean the deck. She glared at Sean. He was not cleaning anything. He was fiddling with a floodlight that did not work. He put batteries in, tried it, took them out, looked at them, and put them in again. She stopped cleaning and watched him.

"You know, Sean, the only way you can make batteries work near water is to lick 'em before you put them into the floodlight," she finally said.

"That's ridiculous. I have a degree in engineering and I've never heard a' such a thing."

Meg baited him, "Okay, have it your way. But if you want that thing to work, you'll have to lick the batteries."

Meg went back to cleaning, but watched Sean out of the corner of her eye. He continued to fiddle with the batteries and became more and more frustrated. Finally, he licked them and put them back into the floodlight. The floodlight still did not work.

Meg burst out laughing, "Gotcha!' I was kidding! I just wanted to see if you'd take directions from me."

She fell down on the deck, howling with laughter.

"You're so not funny, Meg," Sean said with disgust.

Meg howled all the more.

Sean kept Meg occupied as they waited to hear from the attorney. The next night, he invited Meg and Robin over to watch a John Wayne shoot 'em up. They sat on the sofa in the living room. There was the usual overflowing ashtray and KitKat wrappers. They each were munching popcorn from their individual bowls. Sean had his tea, Meg had her Diet Pepsi, and Robin had a regular Coke. (They each had their own drinks of choice, it just wasn't alcohol.)

Sean got up and went into his bedroom. While he was gone, there was a bar room brawl scene in the movie, then a gun shot rang out in the apartment. Meg and Robin screamed, jumped up, and ran into the bedroom.

Sean had a cowboy holster strapped on. A 22-caliber six-shooter was laying on the floor.

Sean looked shocked and bewildered, "I shot me' dresser."

Meg and Robin looked at Sean. Their mouths dropped opened and then they exploded into howls of laughter. They walked over to the dresser and opened it to find Sean's clothes shredded. A huge hole was in the back of the dresser when they pulled it out. They picked up the remains of an elegant angora sweater from Scotland.

"Me' favorite," Sean moaned.

Meg and Robin held their sides, snort laughing.

Sean saw no humor in the situation.

The phone was ringing when Meg rushed in the door from work. She grabbed it.

"Hello," she said, then she listened, "They what?" she paused, "Are you sure? Oh my God. Oh my God."

She hung up the phone and ran out the door, jumped in her car, and drove away. Moments later she pulled up in front of Sean's apartment. She raced to the door and rang the bell non-stop.

She was breathless, "I had to tell you in person. They dropped the case!"

Sean held the door, "What?"

Meg pushed past him and rushed inside his apartment as she babbled, "The Federal Grand Jury dropped the criminal aspects of my case. I don't have to go in front of them, they dropped the felony charges. I won't go to prison or jail even!"

Sean hid his huge relief and gave her a hug, "Of course, Meg, I expected this. It's your typical AA miracle. Your part was ta' not drink and go ta' meetin's, and God did the rest. This is just a regular example of God doin' for us what we cannot do for ourselves.

"Now, why don't ya' go home and get dressed in your meetin' clothes and I'll pick ya' up and take ya' out for a big steak dinner with a shrimp cocktail, and then we'll go to a meetin' and share this experience, strength, and hope with others."

Meg agreed and headed out the door. She came back to give Sean one more huge hug. As soon as he got her out the door, he rushed toward the phone, tripping on the cord and almost falling. He quickly dialed Abbey's number.

"Hello."

Sean was exhilarated, "Abbey, it's a fuckin' miracle! She's off the hook."

"What are you talking about?"

"Meg's not goin' ta' jail. They dropped the case," Sean screamed in the phone.

"They who?"

"The Federal Grand Jury."

"Sean, are you sure?"

"Damn it ta' hell, Abbey, yes!"

"Thank God," she said as she slid down the wall, tears of relief streaming from her eyes.

Sean and Meg went to dinner and the meeting. They were wearing their customary jeans, white button down Oxford cloth shirts, boots, and cowboy hats. After the meeting, they were upbeat as members of the group who had been sharing the drama with Meg came up, gave their well wishes, and hugged her. Abbey and Robin were especially thrilled and relieved for her. Sean dropped her off at her apartment. She watched him go.

She went inside but was too keyed up to stay. She decided to drive around. The radio was on full blast; she sang along. She turned into the driveway of a recovery hospital that was nearby. She went inside and explained to one of the nurses why she was there.

"So, just by staying sober, I've had this incredible miracle and I want to give back. Is there someone here I can help?"

The nurse was touched by Meg's sincerity and nodded "yes" as she led her down the hall outside one of the rooms.

"This young woman is in detox. She was in an automobile accident. All you will be able to do is hold her hand," the nurse said.

Meg nodded yes. The nurse took her inside the room where the woman was asleep, bandaged with a broken left arm and cuts on her face. The nurse pulled up a chair for Meg. She sat down next to the bed and took the woman's right hand. She sat quietly and watched the woman sleep.

Several weeks later, on a gorgeous autumn afternoon, many members of the group met at the free standing bleachers at the Grandview High School football stadium. Among them were Abbey, Michael, Karen, and Tammie. Meg and Robin lugged camera equipment and a large artist's portfolio to the spot where everyone was meeting. Robin started setting up the equipment with her back to the sun. Meg directed people to sit on the bleachers, making four rows. There was alot of chaos and confusion. No one was paying attention to Meg's direction. Everyone was chattering.

Above the noise, Abbey shouted, "Meg, did you get permission from the school for us to be here?"

Meg rolled her eyes, "Oh please, what are they going to do? Arrest us?"

Meg continued to direct the seating. Robin focused the camera and added to the confusion by also directing. Meg went to the portfolio and pulled out 16 by 20 inch cardboard cards with a single, huge, block letter on each one. She handed them out, five on the top row, ten on the next row down, then eight, and five on the bottom row. There were two cards on the bottom row for Meg and Robin. The extra people filled in around those with the cards. Those with cards held them up and Robin shouted directions for people to move to the left or right, she focused the camera, set the timer, and moved into her place next to Meg.

"Everyone smile!"

The camera flashed and the photo said:

**HAPPY
SEX-TEENTH
BIRTHDAY
SEAN!!!**

A week later, at one of their regular meetings, Sean was at the podium. Everyone applauded. Meg walked up to him with a large, wrapped gift.

"Sean, I want to thank you for sharing your story with us tonight. Luckily, we share one heart to another heart. Otherwise, most of us would not have understood a word you said because of your thick brogue. And to think, you speak English this well after only eighteen years in America." Laughter filled the room, then Meg said, "I am honored to give you this gift from all of us here at your home group as a memento of your 16th AA Birthday."

Sean ripped open the gift. It was a beautifully framed photograph of the group from the football field. This unexpected surprise caught him off guard; he had a lump in his throat. He beamed as he held the photo up for all to see.

―――

Over the summer and into the fall, Meg had been able to connect with Karen, most of the time. They met at meetings and talked every day. When the phone rang that late afternoon, Meg had just stepped out of the shower and was drying her hair.

"Hello."

It sounded like a wounded animal was wailing on the other end of the phone before Karen finally spoke.

"I can't do this one more minute. I'm going to kill myself," Karen gasped.

"I'll be right there. Listen to me Karen, hold on to the phone until I get there. Do you understand me? Karen!" Meg screamed.

Karen did not answer. Meg dropped the phone and left it dangling. She threw on some clothes and rushed out the door. When she got to Karen's, she went in without knocking. She found Karen lying in a fetal position in the corner of the room, holding onto the phone. Karen's eyes were glazed over. Meg made a quick survey of the room and saw razor blades on the floor. She sat down and pulled Karen into her arms.

Meg was frantic, "Did you take any drugs?"

Karen nodded, no.

"I don't want to be here," Karen cried.

Meg rocked her, "I know, Baby, I know."

Meg continued to rock her while she figured out what to do.

"Do you think you can get up?"

Karen struggled to stand; Meg helped her to the car. Meg drove directly to Sean's apartment and got there just as he pulled up from work. They got out of their cars.

"Karen called a few minutes after I got off of work. She is seriously suicidal, much worse than usual. It's more than I can handle," Meg told Sean.

Sean nodded his clear understanding of the situation. He helped Meg get Karen out of the car and into his apartment. They sat Karen down on the sofa. Meg sat a the chair across from the sofa and Sean sat down next to Karen. He fired up a cigarette and offered one to Karen. Her arms were crossed. She refused.

"So Lassie, I understand ya' wanna be dead."

Karen's eyes had cleared somewhat. She looked at Sean with contempt but did not speak. Sean talked to Karen about recovery one day at a time. He was animated and intense as time passed. Karen responded with anger or indifference no matter what he said. Meg looked on and said nothing. She was watching a Master at work.

"God loves ya' Karen. He wants ya' ta' be clean and sober and alive. You've got your whole life ahead a' ya.'"

Karen remained bitter and hostile, "There is no God and if there was, I'd hate him for letting me be born. And I'd hate him even more for making me stay alive. I WANT TO BE DEAD AND YOU CAN'T STOP ME!"

"Are ya' sure that's what ya' want?"

"YES," Karen glared.

Sean got up from the sofa and walked casually over to his briefcase. He flipped it open and took out a 357 Magnum. He checked to see if there were bullets in it, then turned around toward Karen.

Meg stopped breathing.

Sean walked over to Karen and established eye contact with her, then he handed her the gun. Sean's eyes were riveted on Karen.

"Don't shoot yourself in the foot."

Meg was frozen, she clutched the arms of the chair. Karen held the gun and continued to look at Sean. He did not flinch. He remained calm and steady. Karen held the gun for a very long time. The stand off continued. Finally, Karen gently laid the gun down on the coffee table and began to sob. Meg went to her and comforted her. She watched Sean pick up the gun and put it away. He was unshaken by the interaction.

Sean and Meg took Karen to a meeting. There was a newcomer at the meeting, Bobby Joe, and he had a teddy bear under his arm. Several of the men at the meeting made it a point to speak to him, including Sean. They all went to the coffee shop after the meeting. Then, Sean and Meg took Karen home and returned to his place. Sean had his hot tea and a cigarette; Meg was drinking a Diet Pepsi. They both were munching on KitKats.

"How could you give her that gun?"

"I knew God would protect us." Sean got up and got the gun out of his briefcase. He showed Meg that it wasn't loaded. He grinned, "And it helps to make sure the gun ain't loaded."

Sean was serious. "Meg, there's no room for half measures in AA. It's how I live this program--all or nothin.' But sometimes common sense must prevail."

As the months passed, Meg grew closer to the program of recovery and more committed to helping others. There was one particular AA event that she had planned and looked forward to for months, The 50 Year International Convention of Alcoholics Anonymous in Montreal, Canada, over the Fourth of July weekend, 1985.

Sean was fast walking toward the departure gate at the Port Columbus Airport. He was in his usual attire, jeans, button down shirt, boots, and a cowboy hat. He was also wearing a very expensive leather jacket and sunglasses. He took a drag off his cigarette as he walked along. Meg was running behind him dragging three bags and a purse. She was sweaty and flushed. She also wore jeans, a button down shirt, and boots. They arrived at the gate as the announcer was making the last boarding call for the flight.

"All passengers should now be on board Flight 1032 for Montreal, Canada," the announcer said.

Sean and Meg handed the flight attendant their boarding passes and made their way to the plane. They moved down the aisle, found their seats, and sat down.
Sean was on Meg's last nerve.

"I can't believe you missed the turn to the airport and got another speeding ticket," she huffed.

Sean was calm, relaxed, and amused by Meg's frazzled condition. He fired up a cigarette and took a drag.

"Relax Meg, there's no reason ta' be a basket case. We made the flight, didn't we?"

She glared at him. She tried to fit all of her bags under the seat. Sean does not offer any assistance.

"Do ya' think ya' brought enough stuff for the weekend?"

"We're going to be there four days," she said defensively.

The flight went smoothly and arrived ahead of schedule. When they got to the opulent hotel lobby, it was already packed with people. Those who were already checked in were wearing tags with their first name, and their city, state, and country beneath it. Sean started talking with people, Meg stood in line to check them in. Robin walked up to Sean.

"I made it! Do we have our room yet?"

"Meg's checking us in now."

Meg joined them with keys in her hand and answers.
She was very pleased with herself. "Yep, we have a mini-suite with two queen-sized beds, just like I was promised."

The chaos in the lobby was intense. People from all over the world greeted each other. A few minutes later, they made their way to the room. It was the size of a matchbox with two twin beds and a tiny bathroom. Meg was crushed.

"Sean, call the front desk. There must be some mistake. I made our reservations six months ago."

Sean sat down on one of the twin beds and fired up a cigarette. He picked up the phone and made the call. Robin and Meg looked over the tiny accommodations.

"Well group, there are no more rooms at the inn, so we'll have ta' make the best of it." He bounced on one of the twin beds. "This is where I'm sleepin,' you girls will have to fight over the other bed."

The phone rang, Sean answered.

"Sure, come on up. We're in room 1248."

"Who was that?" Meg asked.

"Tommy and Diane. They have no place to stay, so I told them they could bunk with us."

"What? Where are they going to sleep?" Meg was freaking out.

"Don't worry, Lassie, they brought sleepin' bags."

"Well, I can't sleep on the floor," Robin said.

"I'm definitely not giving up my bed," Meg said.

Sean watched them, amused.

"Then we'll have to share it," Robin said.

"Fine, but no touching," Meg said.

"Fine," Robin said.

There was a knock at the door. Tommy and Diane came in with all of their gear and threw it in the corner.

"We better check in at the convention center right now because tomorrow it will be mobbed."

They all headed out the door.

The scene at the convention center registration area was overwhelming. Thousands of people from all over the world mingled.

"Whata ya' say we go over ta' the sports arena where they're havin' a dance," Sean said.

As they headed out, they saw many of their friends from Ohio. Amid the commotion, Sean saw John and Dave carrying their suitcases and sleeping bags.

"Sure, we're in room 1248. Here's my key. Just drop off your stuff and meet us at the dance," Sean said.

People with name tags were everywhere as they walked to the sports arena. It was a massive sea of recovery; people stopped, said hello, smiled and waved to one another as they passed.

When they got to the dance it was packed with more than 5,000 sober people. Live bands played at both ends of the arena. People were everywhere. Sean and Meg walked through the crowd around the rim of the arena. The music and noise were deafening.

"Meg, there are millionaires who'd give everything they have ta' feel what we're feelin.' All their money can't buy 'em sobriety," Sean said with intensity, "this is the miracle, the incredible Grace of God, ta' be here sharin' the 50th Anniversary of the program with 50,000 sober al-key-holics."

Meg and Sean danced with each other and everyone around them. It was a joy-filled night.

It was crowded when they all got back to the hotel room. Sean was relaxing on his bed, smoking a cigarette. Tommy, Diane, Dave, and John spread their sleeping bags out where ever they could on the floor.

Meg sat on the other twin bed, waiting for her turn in the tiny bathroom. Robin was in the bathroom brushing her teeth. There was a knock at the door. And since no one else offered to answer it, Meg carefully stepped around the bodies on the floor to get to the door.

She opened it. The man standing outside with his suitcase was Bobby Joe. He was wearing a cap with a gob of crap on it and holding a huge teddy bear. He grinned at Meg. She looked at him, she did not speak, then slammed the door in his face.

"Who was that, Meg?" Sean asked as Meg made her way back to the bed.

"Bobby Joe and his teddy bear, looking for a place to stay," she replied, matter-of-factly.

"Well, I'm glad to see that bein' here has given ya' such a spiritual edge. You're a tribute ta' humanity."

Meg ignored him. Robin came out of the bathroom. She and Meg stood by the tiny bed. Sean and the others were watching.

"Remember, no touching!" Meg said.

"Fine with me," Robin replied.

They got into the bed, struggled with the covers, and of course, they touched. They looked at each other and burst into laughter.

The next morning, Robin took a picture of all of them crowded together on one of the twin beds. It was an historic record of this amazing shared adventure.

Their experiences over the next four days were extraordinary. Sharing meetings with people from all over the world, hearing the Serenity Prayer said in unison in many languages was breathtaking.

When they weren't in meetings, the gang took a grand tour of the area. They went to the Montreal Museum of Fine Arts and saw a breathtaking Picasso exhibit. Dave shared a story about the great artist. Once an interviewer had discussed the artist's career which was very traditional in his early work and often people said, "Oh my child could do that," of his later work. Picasso had replied, "Oh, monsieur, it takes a very long time to become young!"

They walked through the shopping district. Sean stopped in an expensive jewelry store and told Meg to wait outside. She spoke to everyone with a name tag. He came out with a gift for her, silver earrings. She immediately put them on. They glistened in the sun and made Meg feel very special.

Next, they all stopped at a men's clothing store to pick outfits for Sean and Tommy. The salesman was very swishy and dramatic. He picked out mauve baggy pants and matching jacket with a deep mauve silk shirt for Sean. Tommy's outfit was deep purple pants and shirt accented with a flowered jacket. The guys were very skeptical, but with the oohs and aahs from their entourage, they bought the outfits. Robin snapped photos of the looking like they were models for a men's fashion magazine.

"Ah Monsieurs," he said with a thick French accent, the fingers of his right hand to his lips, throwing a kiss, "Exquisite!"

Sunday morning the stadium filled with more than 50,000 sober people for the final meeting. The gang was together in the stands. Chants of "Sober, Sober, Sober," began and the crowd did waves to the chants. At the end of the meeting, they said the Our Father prayer. Meg clearly asked for "jelly bread" and Sean's eyes filled with tears when he heard her. He gazed at her with such joy.

As people were saying the last part of the prayer, a blind woman stepped up to the bank of microphones in the middle of the field. She touched the microphones to establish her distance from them, and then in pure, bellowing tones, she sang "Amazing Grace" unaccompanied.

There was not a dry eye in the stadium.

Back in Columbus, Meg was sharing her story at the Friday North Group Speakers Meeting. Sean was in the audience, very enthusiastic. He was sitting next to his new girlfriend, Amy, a lovely, petite blonde with blue eyes. Karen, Robin, and Abbey were also there. While she was speaking, Warren walked into the back of the room. Meg gasped when she saw him and lost her place for a moment. She quickly regained her composure.

"Being in Montreal with 50,000 sober alcoholics was an experience beyond words. What an incredible gift this is to have found AA. I'm so grateful to be a sober alcoholic. That's something I never thought I'd say. And I thank God for every one of you in these rooms. Thanks for asking me to share."

Everyone applauded; Warren clapped especially loudly. He went up to Meg and gave her a long, loving hug, then he slipped something into her pocket and whispered, "I'm back to stay this time, Darling."

As Meg was getting ready for bed, she remembered Warren had given her something. She got her jacket, reached in the pocket, and pulled out the Recovery Rock.

Tears filled her eyes as she read it. It said: The Program Works If You Work It.

The days of summer passed by quickly. Sean and Amy went to meetings, to dinner, and to spend time on his boat. She wore skimpy bikinis and drove the boat while he water skied behind it, always waving an arm and showing off. She would spend the night and happily take his laundry home. Amy had fallen for him--hard.

***

Meg was spending time with Warren doing the things he liked doing, going to the theatre, the opera, the ballet. He would hold her hand and make her feel special. She would spend the weekends at his place and he would serve her breakfast in bed. One morning, a small black box was on the tray with a single red rose.

"We've waited too long, Meg. I want you to be my wife," he said.

Amy and Sean sat on his sofa making out. The coffee table was covered with the usual overflowing ashtray and KitKat wrappers. A basket of dirty laundry sat in the middle of the living room floor. They made their way into the bedroom for the night.

Sean was in the kitchen the next morning smoking a cigarette, leaning against the counter, when Amy bounced in, smiling. She looked refreshed in a white shirt tied at the waist, jeans miniskirt, and barefoot. She sidled up to Sean to kiss him for last night's pleasure. He barely kissed back, made only brief eye contact, and looked over her shoulder. She did not think, she reacted by hitting him in the chest as hard as she could.

"I don't get it! We have amazing moments where...," she sighed and paused and looked at him, "and then I hit a brick wall."

Sean was silent, pulled inward, still puffing his cigarette. Tears of frustration filled Amy's eyes.

"Who hurt you so bad that you're so afraid to love?" Amy said.

Sean turned white, his eyes glazed over.

"Well, I give up darlin.' My best shot just ain't good enough."

Amy looked at Sean tenderly, she glided her hand down his cheek, along his neck down to his shirt collar. Sean was frozen. She turned away from him, grabbed her keys and purse, and slid on her shoes. The basket of dirty laundry was still on the living room floor where it had been the night before. Amy walked around it as she went to the door. She turned and looked at Sean one last time.

"I hope you find her one day," she said with controlled emotion, "that one with the key."

Amy walked out the screen door; it slammed behind her.

Sean did not watch her go. He was staring downward, a frozen, smoking statue.

―――∽―――

Sean called Meg and said she was to meet him for dinner at The Claremont. They munched their shrimp cocktails. He had his hot tea and a burning cigarette in the ashtray. Meg was babbling.

"Oh everything's wonderful with Warren. Ever since we got engaged, he's been treating me like a princess. I always knew we'd end up together. So, how's it working out with Amy?"

Sean fired up another cigarette and shook his head.

"Not good. I guess I don't understand women. Every time I start datin' a girl, she gets serious way too fast. What am I doin' wrong, Meg?"

"Laundry," Meg answered matter-of-factly.

Sean looked surprised by her answer.

"When you ask a woman to do your laundry, she starts thinking about the laundry room in the little white house with the white picket fence."

"But I hate doin' m' own laundry." Sean paused and was thoughtful, he took a drag off of his cigarette, "So, you can do it from now on."

Meg was not thrilled.

The following weekend, Meg and Warren joined Sean and his new girlfriend, Jenny, on his boat. Jenny was a lovely, athletic young woman with blonde hair and brown eyes. They all looked tan and healthy except for Sean who was more red than tan. Sean drove the boat as fast as it would go. They all held on for dear life, laughing.

Later that night, they all went bowling. Sean and Meg whooped it up. When Sean rolled a strike, Meg clapped, cheered, and jumped up and down. Jenny and Warren sat with their arms crossed looking very bored.

They all converged at a speaker's meeting several days later. Meg, Warren, Jenny, Robin, Tommy, Diane, Karen, Dave, John, Wendy, and Bobby Joe, without his Teddy Bear, were there. Sean was telling his story. Meg had asked Sean early on why did she have to hear the same speaker more than once and he said, "Because hopefully you will have grown and the speaker will have grown as well."

He was lively and animated that night.

"...Ya' know, I don't hold myself up as any good example of Alcoholics Anonymous. I stay sober sometimes and I wonder how the hell I do it, 'cause today I don't feel I have as intense an awareness as I did my first two years in the program. I guess it's like anything else. In the first two years, if I had a problem, I went ta' the Big Book ta' find the answer and a lot of what I read, over the years, has become instinct with me. But even today, if I get too hungry, angry, lonely, or tired, and I feel like m' ass is fallin' off, I go ta' the Big Book, and I call people up. Ya' know, I've got m' friend, Meg. We met each other about two and a half, three years ago, and she was another basket case when she first came in. And I've watched her grow, and it's been a great gift ta' me. Meg and I are really close. I call her up and dump all my crap on her, and Meg calls me up and dumps all her crap on me. And I can tell Meg anything about me and know she can help me. But, I have to let her know what's really goin' on with me."

He paused.

"After a while, it's not a sponsor-pigeon relationship. We've just become good friends."

After the meeting, they all went to Friendly's.

After everyone else had left, Sean and Meg decided to go for a bike ride. It was a perfect night to ride the wind. They rode his Harley at breakneck speed down their favorite dirt road in the star light.

Meg did not wear a helmet.

※

Meg's apartment was neat and clean. She was in the living room, the television was on, she was talking with Warren and holding the phone between her head and left shoulder. She stood at the ironing board, ironing Sean's blue ruffled shirt. A dozen Oxford cloth, button down shirts were neatly pressed and on hangers, hanging from one of the chairs. The front door was opened, a breeze came through the screen door. Sean walked up and Meg motioned for him to come in.

"Gotta go, Darling, Sean's here."

Sean was extremely upbeat.

"Hell-ooo Missy! How ya' doin' with m' laundry?"

"You are a royal pain in the ass," she replied jokingly, "the Oxford cloth shirts are bad enough, but why do you have to wear this stupid blue ruffled shirt every single week?"

"It brings out the blue in m' eyes, Luv! Have ya' had supper?"

Meg shook her head no. Sean reached in his pocket and pulled out a $20 bill.

"How 'bout gettin' us some fish and chips."

Meg put down the iron, picked up the cash, and headed out the door. Sean changed the television channels until he found a John Wayne shoot 'em up."

When Meg returned with the bag of food, Sean was just finishing ironing the blue ruffled shirt. He put it on a hanger and smiled. Their eyes met. Meg caught her breath.

Sean's latest squeeze, Jenny, had asked Meg to meet her for lunch. She wanted to know what her chances were with Sean.

"You may not like what I'm going to tell you, but I'll tell you the truth," Meg said, "I've known Sean a long time. He's my best friend."

Meg paused before she continued.

"If you're dating him to have fun and be in the moment, you're definitely with the right guy. He's a blast. But if you're looking for more, forget it. He's just not the marrying kind."

Jenny had tears in her eyes. "But I'm in love with him."

Meg was sensitive to her feelings, "Oh Jenny, you're setting yourself up for a world of hurt if you think you can get more from Sean than he can give."

Meg was being fitted for her wedding dress. Her dream was coming true. The seamstress was pinning the hem when Warren appeared.

"Darling, what are you doing here?" she bubbled.

"I wanted to see you," he said flatly.

Meg went behind a dressing room curtain and peeked out at Warren. She was giddy.

"It's bad luck for you to see me now, Silly. Anyway, I have so much to do before I go to Tampa for my job interview at the college on Monday. You will take me to the airport, won't you?"

"Why don't we just fly off to Bimini tonight, like the old days, and never look back?" Warren said.

"Like the old days? Are you crazy? We were too drunk to even see Bimini in the old days. Why don't we talk tomorrow? I'll have lots of time then. I love you so, my Darling," she said, throwing him a kiss.

"Goodbye Meg," Warren said deliberately.

He left the bridal shop.

Sean's alarm clock said 7 a.m. The phone was ringing. He answered it and immediately showed panic. He fired up a cigarette, slammed down the phone, dressed and rushed out the door. Moments later he pulled up to the Jai Lai Lounge and rushed inside. The harsh morning light streamed through the dirty windows. Several people sat on bar stools. Sean looked around and his eyes focused on the Scotch whiskey among the bottles behind the bar.

Meg bounced into her regular Friday noon meeting. Sean's line had been busy when she called at 7 a.m., but she knew she would see him at the meeting. There was a solemn air about the room as people talked quietly. A hush fell on the room when she entered. She did not notice it.

"Where's Sean?"

No one spoke. People looked at each other with dread. John walked toward her.

"Oh my God, you don't know," he said.

"Know what?"

The emotion on John's face frightened her. Everyone in the room was speechless. He put his hands on her shoulders, hesitated, and blurted out, "Warren's dead."

"That's not funny. Stop it!" Meg said.

"It's true, Meg. Warren's dead," his eyes filled with tears.

Meg screamed and fell into John's arms. He pulled her close to his chest. Other members came up and offered comfort and support. Meg fell to the floor, sobbing uncontrollably.

Sean crashed into the room and scooped Meg into his arms. He motioned to the others to give them a little space. He held her and rocked her, his face was filled with pain.

Sean took Meg to his apartment, sat her on the sofa, and wrapped her up in his Scottish plaid blanket. Her eyes were swollen, but her tears had lessened. He got her a Diet Pepsi, then fixed a grilled cheese sandwich, some canned chicken soup, the extent of his culinary abilities, and a KitKat. Sean showed her such tenderness.

When it was time to leave for the Friday night meeting, Sean put her in the car and drove. Meg was mostly numb and showed no expression.

"Warren got drunk. Blind drunk. He had ta' stop the voices, so he picked up a gun and blew his head off. The insanity of alcoholism is what killed him, Lassie."

Meg was silent.

After the meeting, Sean said Meg was spending the night at his place. He made her a comfy bed on the sofa. He tucked her in and waited until she finally fell asleep.

He went into his bedroom, but he could not sleep. He stared at the ceiling. He fired up a cigarette, took a few drags and ground it out in the ashtray by his bed. He got up and walked back into the living room. He leaned over Meg and watched her sleep. He knelt down and lovingly touched her hair.

The next night, Sean drove Meg to the funeral home.

"Sean Patrick, what is the point of this kind of pain," she asked.

"So ya' can walk through it with dignity--sober. Not drinkin' is just a footnote ta' livin' a sober life, Lassie," his eyes softened, "When ya' get ta' the other side a' the pain, you'll have a little bag a tools ta' help someone else in this kind a' pain. But ya' have a job today. You're ta' offer comfort ta' Warren's mom and dad."

As they walked into the funeral home, many familiar faces from the meeting rooms were there, both outside and inside the building. They greeted Meg with warmth and care.

Once inside, Meg went to Warren's mother. She dissolved into Meg's arms and Meg held her and spoke softly to her. Sean stayed by Meg's side.

Meg took a deep breath and made her way to the closed mahogany casket, covered with a blanket of roses. Sean stood back. He watched her kneel down and lean into the casket; her body shook with quiet sobs. She stood up and placed something among the flowers on top of the casket.

It was the Recovery Rock that said: *The Program Works If You Work It.*

She turned and walked to Sean, she put her head on his shoulder, he put his arm around her, and they left together.

Part Five

The community college had graciously rescheduled Meg's interview, and they did offer her the teaching job at the Tampa campus. Meg was packing her things for her move to Florida when Sean showed up to help her. Boxes were everywhere, but she made a space on the floor for them to sit. She got a Diet Pepsi and served him a cup of tea with five sugars. He fired up a cigarette.

"You're gonna be a wonderful teacher."

"I'm still believing in you believing in me. My heart still hurts and I'm scared to be so far away from you." She paused and choked up, "How could I have been so stupid to love Warren all those years?"

Sean took her hand and looked into her eyes.

"Ya' weren't stupid, Lassie. Suicide is the act of alcoholic insanity. This disease is just too big for us without a God of our understanding. I promise ya,' Meg, when ya' get ta' the other side of your anger and pain, you'll have a gentle understanding. You'll be able ta' forgive Warren and move on with your life. He was in alot of misery. When ya' come into AA ya' must admit you're an alkie. Then it takes a while to accept yourself as an alkie. But ya' don't find any happiness until ya' approve of yourself being an alkie."

Sean paused and breathed deeply.

"Warren was never able to admit he was an al-key-holic. He never got this Program."

Sean got up and went to the place where his coat was laying. There was a sack beside it and he pulled out a beautifully wrapped box. He handed it to Meg.

"Here's a little somethin' so ya' won't forget me," he grinned.

Meg was excited; she tore open the box. Inside was the blue ruffled shirt, neatly pressed and folded. She burst out laughing.

"How I hated ironing this shirt!" She pulled it to her chest, "I'll treasure it."

She sat the shirt down and looked away. She pretended to be packing.

"Sean, you've had a lot of girlfriends since I've known you. And I was just wondering..."

She hesitated.

"What Meg? Ya' know ya' can ask me anything."

"I was just wondering if you ever thought of me, you know, like you would think of a girlfriend? Like I was appealing that way?"

He glanced away, fired up a cigarette and took a deep drag.

"Meg, that day that ya' asked me ta' be your sponsor, I prayed ta' God ta' block those feelin's from me. I knew I couldn't help ya' stay sober if I was sleepin' with ya.' And, God answered that prayer," Sean was sure he had convinced her.

She looked into his eyes, "I love you, Sean Patrick, promise you'll come and run the beach with me."

"I promise," he said softly.

Sean forced a smile, she buried her head in his chest and hugged him. His eyes filled with tears as he held her and kissed her hair.

Meg stood barefoot on the sandy beach outside her new home, a bungalow with a huge picture window overlooking the ocean. Moving boxes could be seen stacked high inside. She wore shorts and T-shirt. A breeze blew through her hair. She began to fast walk, then she ran at full speed down the beach out of sight.

Her new home was the perfect haven for her to write. She set up her typewriter at a desk in front of the picture window looking out at the ocean. She had hung up a beautifully framed, handmade cross-stitch of the Serenity Prayer, and an eight by ten framed photo of Sean and her. She was straightening the photo when the phone rang.

"Hello," she said.

"Howdy Little Missy. What's goin' on?"

"Sean, I just hung up a photo of you and me," she squealed, "it's in a very special place right next to our favorite Prayer. How are you?"

Sean had his hot tea with five sugars and a KitKat bar in front of him. The usual overflowing ashtray had long cigarettes in it that had been crushed out after only one drag.

"Fantastic!" he lied convincingly.

"Guess what? There's a meeting on the beach about half a mile from my place called the Sunset Group. I've already made it my home group. I can't wait 'til you get here to go with me. Imagine! I'm living on the beach and I go to sleep at night listening to the ocean. It's incredible."

"Great, Meg."

"Will you be coming to visit soon?"

"Yes, Pigeon 847. Soon."

"Oh, I've got to go or I'll be late for my meeting. Bye Sean. Love you!"

"Bye Lassie," he said softly. He ground out a cigarette in the overflowing ashtray. Sadness filled his eyes.

She was at the Sunset Group meeting, everyone sat in a circle on blankets on the sand. Meg was connecting to her new sobriety family. It was a discussion meeting and as the comments went around, people were laughing and animated. They stood for the "Our Father" at the end of the meeting.

After the prayer, a very handsome man around her age, Sam, asked, "Did you say 'Jelly Bread?'"

Meg grinned, "It's a long story."

Sam asked her to an all night cafe near the meeting so he could hear the 'long story.' They sat at a table outside. Meg ordered a Diet Pepsi, Sam had coffee. They talked and laughed until late into the night.

Meg's alarm went off. She opened her eyes, got out of bed, and got down on her knees. Several weeks had passed since she had talked with Sean. She picked up the phone and dialed.

"Hell-o."

"Sean, it's Meg. It's 7 a.m. and I was missing you. So I'm calling to say good morning just like old times."

"Good mornin' Lassie, I miss ya' too. I'll see ya' before ya' know it. Have a fantastic day."

Sean smiled as he put down the receiver. Meg rushed to get dressed and out the door for work.

Saturday was a glorious day. Meg spent it parasailing with Sam. He was so different than Warren; he was open and warm and real. She was able to be herself without wondering what he wanted her to be. Their relationship was growing into more than a friendship.

Now, she sat at her typewriter, working and watching a spectacular sunset out her living room window. Her new home was spotless, everything was in its place. Her face was serene.

The following week Meg was relaxing and watching the seagulls wander aimlessly on the beach. She was wearing shorts and Sean's blue ruffled shirt with the sleeves rolled up. There was a knock at the door, and she got up to answer it. She flung open the door, and Sean was standing there with a broad smile on his face. He was wearing his familiar garb, jeans, Oxford cloth, button down shirt, boots, cowboy hat, and shades. His white Lincoln was parked in front of Meg's home with his Harley on the trailer attached behind it. He handed her a box of KitKats and a carton of Diet Pepsi.

"I just happened to be in the neighborhood so thought I'd drop by an' say Howdy," he chuckled, "like your shirt!"

Meg was thrilled to see him. She grinned as she took the gifts and sat them down as he came inside. She turned to hug him and Sean lifted her off the ground.

"I'm so glad to see you. I thought you weren't coming until spring. This is the very best surprise!"

Sean looked around the bungalow, then stood in front of the picture window.

"It's a great place, Meg," he said.

She put a teapot on the stove and got down the tea bags and sugar; she took an ashtray out of the cupboard.

Meg took Sean outside and pointed up and down the beach. They came back in and Sean made his tea. At dusk, they walked to the beach meeting. Sean carried his plaid blanket and laid it down for them. She introduced him to Sam. Sean sized Sam up before having a conversation with him. After the meeting, the three of them went to the nearby cafe for coffee, tea, and Diet Soda.

"Seems like a great guy," Sean told Meg later.

When Sean and Meg got back to her place, he brought his bike around to the beach. Meg climbed aboard. He revved the motor and took off down the beach. The full moon lit the sky, the stars glittered like diamonds.

They stopped, pulled off their shoes, ran into the waves, laughing and splashing one another. Meg stumbled, but Sean caught her before she fell. He pulled her close and hugged her. He kissed her full on the mouth. She kissed him back. They looked into each others eyes, speechless.

Sean was asleep on the sofa the next morning when Meg came out of her bedroom wearing shorts and a T-shirt. She put on the coffee and water for Sean's tea. She sat down and watched him sleep.

"Good morning, Sleepy Head. I called work and took the next two days off. Thought we could do some sight seeing," Meg said when Sean opened his eyes.

"Fantastic!"

Neither of them mentioned the kiss.

They rode "the Hog" on wonderful back country roads between Tampa and Orlando. The wind blew through their hair, the sun sparkled above them. They rode back to Meg's and went to the beach.

In the early evening, they walked past the boardwalk to an elegant carousel. The horses were beautifully hand carved and painted. Sean tipped his hat to Meg as she climbed on one of the horses. His long legs dangled and touched the ground as the horses moved up and down. When they got off the carousel, he took Meg's hand.

"I need ta' talk ta' ya, Luv."

"Sure."

They sat down under a nearby cypress tree.

"I wanted ta' tell ya' this in person." He looked into her eyes, "Meg, I've got lung cancer. It's inoperable. The doctors are goin' ta' start treatments next week."

Meg was shocked; she was quiet, trying to conceal her emotions. She chose her words carefully.

"We'll beat this thing together, Sean," she said upbeat and confident. "Look at all we've already been through. God didn't bring you this far to give up on you now."

She smiled at him and took his hand. They sat quietly watching the waves crash onto the beach.

Although Meg talked to Sean every other day, she had not seen him in almost eighteen months. She was going back to Columbus for her AA birthday and was thrilled to be seeing him, especially since he said he had an enormous surprise for her.

When Meg got off the plane at Port Columbus Airport, Sean was waiting for her, holding five roses. He looked vibrant, healthy. She beamed when she saw him and gave him a long hug.

"It's about time ya' got here," he said.

"Like I could make the plane go faster," she retorted.

He handed her the roses.

"Five years. It's a miracle!"

They both laughed.

"You look wonderful. Another miracle?"

Sean nodded yes.

"Total remission," he said.

They hugged again.

They went to Sean's place, went to dinner, and then went to the Friday North Group meeting where Sean had forced her to shake hands with everyone in the beginning. Several hundred people were there. Meg greeted all her friends; they shared hugs and love and laughter. Sean went to the podium.

"It is my great honor to present a five year medallion ta' a very special friend of mine. I remember when she first came into the program. She was a real mess." Everyone laughed. Sean continued, "I didn't think she'd make six months back then, and here she is, five years clean and sober. Shows what I know. This Lassie and I have been through a lot together. And we're always there for one another. She knows me better than anyone in the world. My heart smiles when I think of her. I give you Meg O."

Meg stood up to thunderous applause. She looked at her sobriety family, many were crying. People began standing up. By the time she reached the podium, the entire audience was giving her a standing ovation. When she reached Sean, he put a medallion in her hand and gave her a hug. She stood in front of her peers, Sean was by her side, tears streamed down her face.

Meg took a deep breath and swallowed.

"I did not realize how much this would mean to me until this very moment. I hope, if you're new, you'll stick around to find a *God of your understanding*. I did, and I found Him in you. And there came a moment when I knew that my God loved me perfect before the earth was made, He loved me perfect my worst day ripping and running, and He loves me perfect right this moment. He doesn't love me more today, because He always loved me perfect.

But I think it pleases Him that I'm clean and sober."

She looked at Sean, "Sean, I believe that God brought you to Columbus because He knew how much I needed you. I love you."

"Thank you, Lassie," he whispered.

The applause was deafening.

Meg returned to Florida after her glorious visit to Columbus. Over the next year, her life was full. She loved her job at the college teaching writing. She wrote every day and was finishing a children's book series. She loved her AA meetings and not only was sponsoring other women, but she helped start a new meeting for women. She was dating Sam. They shared sobriety and helping others was a priority for both of them. And Meg was falling in love with him. She thought about Sean every day, prayed for him every day, and talked with him as often as she could.

It was a perfect Florida spring day. When Meg entered her apartment after an early morning swim in the ocean, the phone was ringing. She answered it unhurried. She was upbeat.

"Hello."

It was Sean; he said with difficulty, "Meg, the cancer's back. I'm in the hospital. It's eatin' up m' spine."

Her hand shook as she held the phone, she swallowed hard, and said calmly, "I'll be right there."

She gently put down the receiver. She was filled with pain and disbelief, tears filled her eyes. She went into the bedroom and quickly dressed in jeans and an Oxford cloth button down shirt. She pulled down a small suitcase with unflappable determination. She packed an extra pair of jeans and a shirt. Fifteen minutes later she was on her way to the airport.

When Meg walked into the hospital, she went directly to Sean's room. A nurse tried to stop her.

Meg was calm, deliberate, she looked the nurse in the eye, "You don't understand, I'm supposed to be here."

The nurse stepped aside.

Meg went into Sean's room. She was shocked. Sean was dying. She pulled a chair up by his bed and sat down. She took his hand and gently held it while he slept.

When Sean opened his eyes the next morning, Meg was smiling at him.

"Hey Sleepy Head. I came all this way to see you and you're sleepin.'"

"Well, I didn't expect ya' in the middle of the night." Sean forced a smile.

Meg's eyes were filled with the love she felt for Sean. His expression was clouded with pain and disgust that he was dying.

Meg stayed with Sean. She read from the Big Book and they shared memories and laughter from all the years they had spent together. They focused on the happy times. But when night came, Sean prayed desperately for God to make him well. He grabbed Meg's hand and pulled her close. He looked at her with intensity.

"I never got honest with myself. I never got honest with the women in my life. I never let anyone really know me--except you."

"I know," Meg said softly.

"Promise me ya' won't make the same mistake," he said with even greater emphasis, squeezing her hand, "Promise me!"

Meg nodded and said tenderly, "I promise, Sean, I promise."

They continued to look at one another as though all of their lives had come to this one moment. Meg held Sean's hand. She watched him. His eyes closed and he squeezed her hand. Then he began to recite the Third Step Prayer from the Big Book and The Our Father prayer. Meg joined in.

When they finished, Sean opened his eyes and said, "I didn't get sober to live without my dignity."

"You don't have to. You have a choice. You can go home, Sean," Meg said her eyes filled with love beyond measure.

She fell asleep holding Sean's hand as she sat by the side of his bed. He watched her sleep.

Bright sunlight flooded the room the next morning.

The nurse came in and woke Meg. The nurse fussed over Sean and he showed his disgust. Meg stood back and watched. Finally, she could stand it no longer.

"Could you leave us alone, please?" she said to the nurse.

The nurse looked at Meg and gave her an understanding nod. She walked out of the room. After she left, Meg turned to Sean. She got very close to his face and smiled but did not speak.

"I'm glad ya' came, Lassie."

"Me too."

Meg fluffed his pillows and made sure he was comfortable.

"I'm going home now," she said.

"I know." He paused. "I'm so proud of you. Run the beach for me."

She grinned and nodded yes.

"Ride the wind for me," she whispered.

They breathed in one another.

"I love you Sean Patrick MacIntosh. No matter where you go or where I go. I love you."

"I love you too, Meg. I love you too."

It was the first time Sean had said I love you.

Meg fought back her tears, she kissed him gently. She pulled back, still looking at him. She caught her breath.

"Now get the hell outa here," he said as lightly as he was able.

Meg stepped back slightly. They grinned at one another. She picked up her purse and suitcase. She touched his hand, turned abruptly, and walked out the door.

She did not look back.

Sean watched her go. When she was out of sight, he grimaced in pain.

Meg walked to the elevator and pushed the button. Sean, in great pain, pushed the button for the nurse.

Meg walked to her car.

Sean watched Meg walk to her car from his hospital window. A tear rolled down his cheek. The nurse came in and gave him a shot of morphine.

Meg raced down the wooded road she and Sean had sped down so many times on his motorcycle. She held the steering wheel steadfastly, she stared straight ahead. Tears filled her eyes. She had a lump in her throat; she remembered.

Sean was surrounded by doctors and nurses.

Meg was calm as she went into the airport. When she reached her gate, she handed the flight attendant her boarding pass and entered the plane. She took a window seat and looked out the window. The sunlight cascaded over her face. Tears filled her eyes, she blinked and the tears rolled down her cheeks.

Sean lost vital signs--Code Blue. Those attending him worked frantically. A faint pulse returned; Sean slipped into a coma.

Meg arrived home and stood on the beach in front of her home. It was sunset. She wore the same jeans and shirt she had worn at the hospital that morning. She was barefoot, her hands in her pockets. She began to walk. She pulled her hands out of her pockets and began to fast walk. She broke into a full run, embracing life.

Sean looked peaceful. He saw himself healthy and vibrant riding full throttle on the Harley with Meg down the dirt road they both loved. His heart monitor showed a weak pulse; it beat slowly four or five times. The monitor flat lined.

Meg burst down the beach in the brilliance of the sunset as it glimmered on the ocean. She saw herself on the same Harley ride, holding tightly onto Sean.

They rode the wind.

FINAL THOUGHTS

To all of those in recovery, thinking about getting into recovery, or loving someone with an addiction, this novel is about hope. As long as we're breathing, there's hope.

"If you're new (to recovery), I hope you'll stick around to find a *God of your understanding*. I did, and I found Him in you. And there came a moment when I knew that my God loved me perfect before the earth was made, He loved me perfect my worst day ripping and running, and He loves me perfect right this moment. He doesn't love me more today, because He always loved me perfect. But I think it pleases Him that I'm clean and sober." (Page 151)

For additional information about a 12-Step program contact: www.aa.org

About the Author:

Nancy DeLong, a passionate, motivational communicator, is a college professor and corporate trainer. She currently teaches writing at a local college where she encourages her students to look at themselves, draw from their experiences, and find their own personal power through their writing. She has published several other books including, *I'm Just Sayin;' Bouquets from God, The Red Book; Happy Birthday Jesus, The Very First Holiday,* and *Put Your Biscuits in the Oven and Your Buns in Bed.* She has written several screenplays, *Ride The Wind,* and *One A.* She produced and edited a powerful docudrama, *Snowbabies--The Innocent Victims,* which raised the awareness of the effects of drugs and alcohol on newborns. It has been widely used in classrooms around the United States. She also produced and edited two widely acclaimed industrial films on the disease of alcoholism as a basis for company employee assistance programs dealing with chemical dependency issues. Nancy lives with her family in Lake Mary, Florida, which includes Sinnabon, Spike, and the spirit of Snickers.

What people are saying:

Ride The Wind is mesmerizing. It's a funny, moving, outrageous, and breathtaking novel---an extraordinary treasure.
        Pam McMahon
        Educator

Fasten your seat belt for a quick read. Ride The Wind is the compelling story of a young woman's struggle to conquer her addictions. It demonstrates the transformational power that can come from a faith in God and the love (sometimes tough love) of those who care for us. This story will touch your heart.
        Chris Parker
        Wealth Advisor

I loved Ride The Wind from the first page. I was riveted throughout this entire book. Nancy DeLong is God's gift of hope to all of life's clear path seekers in a world filled with challenges. This novel is a complete winner!
        Donna Wendt
        Humanitarian

I believe Ms. DeLong found her muses in Sean and Meg. This novel reads like a screen play; I see it as an award winning motion picture. Carolyn Litwin
        Pastoral Advisor

Nancy DeLong has written another beautiful story in the language she knows best, the language of the heart! Brilliant!!   Steve Timmer
        Adventurer

Order additional copies today!!

N. GLYNN PUBLISHING

RIDE THE WIND

Send:
- **$9.95 per copy**
  US funds check or money order
  Payable to: N. Glynn Publishing, LLC

Plus:
- Shipping and Handling
  $3.50 for first copy
  $2.00 each additional copy

TO:
N. Glynn Publishing LLC
P.O. Box 951414
Lake Mary, FL 32795-1414
407.324.0337

or visit:
http://www.nancydelong.com

**Other books by Nancy DeLong
also available.** *(See order form)*

N. GLYNN PUBLISHING

QTY	Description	Total
	Ride The Wind $9.95 each	$
	I'm Just Sayin' Volume I $9.95 each	$
	Bouquets from God, The Red Book $9.95 each	$
	HAPPY BIRTHDAY JESUS, The Very First Holiday $19.95 each	$
	Put Your Biscuits in the Oven and Your Buns in Bed $19.95 each	$
	S&H ($3.50 first copy $2.00 additional copies)	$
	Tax (where applicable)	$
	Total:	$

For large orders or credit card contact:
orders@nancydelong.com